AFRO-CUBAN

BOOGIE WOOGIE

BY
LINTON
ROBINSON

Adoro Books is a Division of Escrit Lit LLC
South Carolina
info@adorobooks.com
See more titles at
AdoroBooks.com/bookstore

Published by Adoro Books
South Carolina, USA
Copyright 2011

adoro books.com

CHAPTERS

To Wendy: "La Vaquera"

ONE

Least they don't have a view of the bay, Moss grumped, following Monsieur Fancypants out to the car; showing off his Frenchy tailored uniform and sounding like he learned shiny perfect English in Concierge Academy. No big shock the cruiser is a Citroen, smug little catfish-face wheels, all mousse and white with some medieval badge on the side and trim little Euro lightbar on top, probably got dimmers and pastel colored lights. Just so much more elegant a squad car than your gauche ol' American Ford Vic.

Moss didn't have to try hard to get pissed at this frog cop was just more of the same he'd been stewing on since the shuttle dropped them off at the Cap'd'Argen police station. If that's even what it was, not some boutique for Ikea desks and Braun office equipment outta some design collection. Something about Europe always gave him a case of the ass. Probably because it was fundamentally, historically, whiter than even the whitest shit back in The World. Wouldn't bug Simms a bit, of course. He's probably hoping they have one those catalogs behind the seat like on the plane, order himself some titanium Lauren handcuffs on his iPhone.

And, matter of fact, Simms completely enjoyed being in Europe and would be there full time if he could swing the assignment. Not the Riviera, so much, but definitely Barcelona, Rome, the Adriatic coast. He chatted up the French officer as they wound up out of the quaint cobblestones, then up some steep streets supported by old stonework and increasingly hemmed in by homes with foliage-drenched walls that could have been built by the Knights of Malta or a rogue Avignon pope or two. Further pissing Moss off. Trust

Simms to speak French. Only way he could possibly get any more whitebread was to study talking through his nose.

Geville, the *gendarme,* found Simms an intelligent, informed conversationalist and deferred to him in respect. Thirtyish, handsome in a blankly refined way, London suit and air of controlled power he managed to keep short of arrogance. And whoever he said he was, the Cape cop had a strong impression he was anything but. Probably CIA or Blackwater or some other *jolie folie americaine.* He had no idea how to deal with Moss: a rugged, fit late forties with a dangerous look, like a chained mastiff. A natural prizefighter. One of those veteran types you sized up immediately as either a criminal or cop. He deferred to Moss, also-- *naturalment* we are not racists in this nation--but didn't really care to have anything to do with him whatsoever. This was a man you kept an eye on--from a distance. He would be quite happy when he arrived at the villa and no longer have to share his car with this pair.

As the car climbed above the trees and rooftops of the port, Simms managed to tear himself away from yammering to the local cop about vintage wines or spring fashion lines or whatever, and addressed his partner on mission matters. "So you're pretty sure he'll be there?"

"You pretty sure I give a shit?" Moss glowered. He'd spent a week tracing that mofo, then had to come all the way to the French freakin' Riviera to deal with him, and he kind of hoped he wasn't around, you really want to know.

"I do, actually," Simms said with one of those satin smiles. "I think you're just dying to give him the finger.

Another thing about the man: he was right too damned much.

2

TWO

The Roman style pool wasn't the fashionable sort of thing to be seen in anymore, perhaps explaining why the villa had run cheaper than expected for two weeks in summer. The water lay like an oblong- cut ultramarine among the old stone columns and fragments, the eldritch atmosphere the whole reason for paying such a stiff rent for two weeks in a villa you could barely get to on foot. Its optically flat surface and lichened arches currently served as the setting for two women of much more recent vintage, both beautiful in very different ways. Shawny looked like a blond American showgirl; a strong and lissome figure revealed when she moved in her simple T-shirt and faded dungarees. Fiametta displayed the opposite of those homegirl looks: she was all angles, dark curls, and cappuccino skin stretched over thoroughbred Italian bone structure and meticulously maintained musculature. Her lush figure was revealed by the fact that she was wearing absolutely nothing.

She stared over Shawny's shoulder as the American woman reached up to adjust the complex intertwining of rope that lashed her hands, suspending her like a lovely "Y" between two Corinthian columns. She didn't look at her, just stared at the man across the pool with an anguishing, beseeching vulnerability that brought her sexuality out in a perverse way. Shawny tucked in a final loop of black climbing rope and stepped back to check her work. She took in Fiametta's forlorn expression and spoke to the man over her shoulder. "Wow, she's almost too pretty to shoot."

"She should have thought of that," he said, and continued arranging his equipment.

THREE

Well, yeah, sure, Moss thought, up here you get a view of the harbor. He slipped out of the homo damned Citroen and looked over the far side of the road, a sheer drop-off to a painterly sprawl of tile roofs and gardens running down to the yellow stone buildings at the harbor, the charming bay where yachts hadn't yet pushed out real fishing boats, the twinkle dance of the Mediterranean out past the breakwater, probably built by Caesar or some such fool. He turned to look at the house, what you could see of it over the wall of quarried stone with big wrought iron gates and spills of cedar and jasmine. Nice digs this asshole's holing up in. Exclusive neighborhood, but apparently not exclusive enough. He walked up to the door behind this tailored Citroen cop and knew it was true that he was getting all over walking in there and giving that asshole the finger.

Geville pulled the graceful iron lever that generated understated, graciously informative chimes somewhere inside. He waited, he and Simms both rubbernecking the view of gardens and battlements inside the gate as well as the postcard scenario to seaward. Big old cruise ship poking by out there. Enjoy, suckers.

A slim caretaker came to the inside of the portcullis-looking gate; uncertain age, immaculate slacks, solid navy tie, and soft white shirt. Geville talked to him, but got only stiff headshakes and a stiffer upper lip. He turned to the Americans and told them, "He says his employer has absolutely no desire to talk to his embassy."

Moss fumed, as much at Geville's wimpy attitude and precise diction as getting stood up on the stoop by

4

the asshole inside. Yeah, you speak better English than I do, he thought, let's get your old lady up here, see who does better with Greek. Simms, of course, stepped up behind him, radiating charm and good sense. Moss figured, what the hell, and loomed menacingly behind them both. No dice. But finally Geville, kind of reluctantly to Moss's eye, pulled out a badge and some document in a thin leather sleeve. The caretaker didn't like it one little bit, but he finally unchunked the portmanteau or whatever and let them in.

FOUR

By then the lovely Fiametta had already been shot. And hadn't completely approved of how the shot was done, but models learn not to bother telling photographers anything. Her new pose also had bondage elements, and a lot more searching examination of her gorgeous and expensive body. If her lash-up between the columns invoked a male desire to protect and rescue, to the laying on of consoling and protective hands, this angled exposure and the smoldering disdain in her face might lead the men who examined her layout in the French edition of "Playboy" to be glad she was tied up and harmless. Shawny was doing some subtle brushing on her cheek, sable blusher in one hand and a lensless Nikon body in the other.

The far side of the pool was littered with fabric-draped patio furniture, tripods, black gear cases covered with shipping and airline stickers, a hanging wardrobe, and the usual bric-a-brac of a photo shoot. At the edge of the pool, Doc Hardesty watched the preparations over the tripod supporting the focusing bellows of his Horseman, glancing occasionally at the creeping shadow of a gargoyle that was going to start shading his shot in about ten minutes. Rangy and well-muscled in his forties, Doc was deceptively large, proportioned more like a man far shorter than his six foot, four inches. He had a healthy tan, an obviously very fit physique, and a habitual air of melancholy on his long, coarse-featured face.

He looked up in annoyance as the caretaker entered the pool area from the salon, but his expression went flat when he saw the cop and two Americans behind him. Though nobody would assume that he was any less annoyed. The caretaker looked for Doc's nod, then left briskly by a route that didn't require him to come near the three interlopers. Doc slipped on a pair of helicopter style sunglasses as the WASP smiled his way up to him, kept a veiled eye on the black bruiser leaning in the doorway behind him and staring at him like he wanted to eat his head.

Across the pool, Shawny whipped a robe from behind a column and draped it over the helpless Fiametta, who was treating the newcomers to some highly attractive glares. She stepped to a table just out of their angle of view and buried her hands in a photo bag, rummaging for a lens cap or something. Then froze with her hands in the gadget bag, relentlessly tracking the intruders' every move

Doc turned and bent to examine the ground glass back of the Horseman 8x10 view camera, ignoring Simms as he came carefully up beside him. And stood there a moment, taking in the expensive ruins of the pool garden and the stony glares of the women, before saying, "I like your studio."

"So do I, thanks," Doc said aside, no inflection of interest. "Can I help you find your way out?"

"Actually, I wonder if we could talk."

"I wonder myself. This place was supposed to be private."

"Mr. Hardesty, I'm Dalton Simms. I work for the CIA."

Doc straightened up, turned to him slowly, and sighed. "Well, if you're expecting me to sneer or spit on you..." he motioned at Fiametta, "...notice I'm not much more than an upscale pornographer myself."

"You're a prominent artist," Simms insisted. "The new Helmut Newton, they say. We'd like you to help us out."

"I offered to, but here you still are."

7

Unflustered, Simms said, "They told me you'd be suspicious. Not much of a patriot."

"Let's just say my patriotism is no longer for rent."

"Fair enough. May I show you something before you tell us to leave?"

"Too late: I thought I already got that across."

"It will only take a second and it could mean a great deal to your friends. Maybe life and death."

Doc stared at him. "It's always life and death with you guys, isn't it?"

Moss had moved up within speaking range of Doc, Shawny shifting slightly to keep him lined up, ready to rock. He sneered, "Like you never made a living off people dying."

"Not since I stopped working for governments, I don't. And it wasn't the Cong or FRELIMO or Sandanistas that made it too nasty for me: it was you. CIA, DEA, whatever alphabet you're working this week."

Simms started to speak, but Doc waved him down. "Okay, show me something. Then you leave. Are we agreed?"

"Perfectly, Mr. Hardesty. Thank you for your patience." He motioned to Herman like an M.C. introducing a new act. "My associate, Herman Moss."

Moss walked towards Doc reaching towards his sport coat. Shawny's forearms immediately tensed, and he rolled his eyes at her while pantomiming slow-motion caution. His fingertips dipped inside his lapel and brought out a metal box the size of a deck of cards. Wordlessly, he extended the box until Doc took it, then folded his arms over his chest.

"Thank you, Herman. Mr. Hardesty, examine that object if you'd like."

Doc held the box, giving it the downcast look of a

man who knows that whatever it is, he isn't going to like it. He pulled the lid open and looked inside at a human finger lying on a bed of cotton like a biology specimen. The finger wore a silver ring set with a very complex piece of turquoise.

He held the box up, scanning the contents for a long moment while the two visitors watched him silently, Shawny fidgeted, and the ignored Fiametta pouted provocatively. He gently removed the ring, dropped it into the pocket of his khaki slacks, and snapped the lid shut on the finger before returning it to Simms, saying, "I'm sure disposing of body parts is no problem for you guys."

Moss smirked truculently. "That what you got to say on the subject?"

"It's hers, of course. I don't think even you people could counterfeit a piece of turquoise I'm so familiar with."

Simms was commiserating. "It is hers. But we're pretty sure she's alive. We know where she is and want her rescued. All we ask is that you help us."

"Do you have boxes specially made for carrying fingers around?"

Moss snorted. "You believe this asshole?"

Simms continued, unperturbed. "It came with a demand for prisoner exchange. We don't think they'll give her up even if we comply, and Washington refuses to exchange anyway. They threatened to send "more personal pieces" if we don't. Do you want in on a rescue?"

"So you held a big meeting and had to admit you couldn't possibly pull this off without flying halfway around the world to get help from an aging malcontent."

"You'd know her on sight, she'd trust your voice. Also, she's where it would be hard to infiltrate quickly.

But a photographer of your reputation should be very welcome. We have an invitation for you to do some shooting at a music festival."

"Very flattering. You mentioned 'friends'. Who else is in this?"

"That's the best part. You don't trust us so we deliver up front."

"So more of my loved ones are tied to railroad tracks somewhere?"

"Just this one primetime shitheel," Moss said. "Name of Jimmy Dan Earl."

Doc gave him a look so incredulous as to be a slap in the face. "Jim Dandy?" he asked, smiling slightly, "Needs my help? Or anybody's? Shouldn't you try to make these little scenarios a bit more believable?"

Simms shook his head, "I just found out about it in Rome on my way here. He's working for some people that are about to turn on him. I can get you in, you can get him out. No muss, no fuss."

"All this just to convince me I can trust the Company."

"Well, we figure that once we extract him, Mr. Earl would owe us a little."

"How much?"

"He's got a pretty good reputation for raids, himself. We hope he'll help us with your rescue project."

"And since you've investigated my emotional history so closely, you're sure I won't turn you down."

"You never really know anything about people. Any of us can change."

"Some of us try. But you keep coming along and not letting us."

Shawny, her hands still in the gadget bag, back straight and elbows locked, had been moving around the end of the pool and came up to Doc, careful not to cut off her line on the two agents. "So don't let them not let you."

Doc didn't look at her. "It's Jude."

"Oh, who else? So you grab your guns and go back out to the fights for Our Lady of Perpetual Heartbreak? Come back dead, or depressed because you shot half the third world again and didn't really mean to?"

"I don't see much choice."

"Same choice as always. Stop killing and just take pictures. There are people to do these things."

"And just because I don't want to be doesn't mean I'm not one of them."

"You have a choice, Doc."

He did turn to face her then. "Would I even have that choice if not for Jude? Would I be alive?"

"Doc, it's completely up to you."

"Yeah, looks like it is."

"That isn't what I meant."

"I know. But it's the way it's going to have to be." He turned away, moved closer to Simms, staring at him from behind the dark glass. "So where's Jim Dandy put himself in dire straits these days?"

Simms, having won, was all-inclusive business. "About seventy miles out of a little place called Lucumba. We can be there tomorrow if you have nothing more to ask me about."

"Lucumba." Doc looked down, idly kicked at a leaf on the flagstones. "Great. Africa's always pretty during bush war season."

FIVE

More time I'm on this shot-out continent, the more I just can't believe all that "Mother Africa" shit back home. That's what was running through Herman Moss's mind in the deteriorated back seat of the internally distressed Toyota taxi with rust eating away the gaudy cinema heroes and goofy little voodoo haints painted all over it, probably holding it together. He grimaced under his coat of equatorial African sweat as the cabbie jolted to a halt on the forbidding deadpan of an alleged airstrip forsaken by not only God, but also by any men and animals with a lick of sense. Not even many vegetables were having it. He looked out the cracked, dusty window as the driver cheerfully jabbered, handed him a big bill without expecting to get any change. What's just unbelievable, he thought, is that there are all those black folks in the States thinking it would be a good idea to up and move back over to this shithole.

He pulled himself out of the stifling heat of the Toyota into the withering blast of the sun and looked around. The idea that it was a military installation thoroughly disgusted him: he'd been military once and had some definite standards. Two shacks looked like they were tumbling down in slow motion, probably why those two goats didn't just head on in through where the doors weren't. A Quonset hut had baked to a khaki color and looked like a dinosaur ribcage surrounded by shifting mists of heat distortion: the idea of setting foot inside it made more sweat roll down his pits and crotch. Couple of shot-out light planes over there, doubtful of making the flightline ever again, got unit designations scrawled on them, or maybe ads for some local juju juice. And one each war-surplus Cobra attack helicopter: bad paint, windows sandblasted, little oil soaked into this mustard-colored clay they got so many miles of around here, but it least it looked functional. Not that he'd want to step into it, either. Welcome to Mammy Africa. Next person calls me "African-American", Moss thought, I'll have 'em up against a wall putting them hip to the real deal over here.

He heard the other door slam, that Hardesty asshole getting out. Moss continued to ignore him, could tell the asshole was staying well behind him. Good. He studied the airstrip some more and wasn't all that impressed by the personnel, either. Three young hardheads squatting down to play dominos in the shade of the Cobra, wearing that same shit-color uniform lookin' like a soccer team meeting the Boy Scouts on Halloween. Got themselves real guns, though, huh? Fabrique Nationale assault carbines, or maybe those Yugo copies, clean and oiled and with that certain air of experience. In fact, here one comes now.

As soon as he'd started walking towards them, one of the soldiers had indolently stood and slouched towards him, his rifle slung muzzle down, way they mostly do in this AO. He studied Moss from under his red beret and behind the mirrored lenses of Oakley knock-offs with fake metal frames, but had a second to spare for the cabbie. He swung his carbine up, smooth and casual, to point at the Toyota and it immediately spun around on bald tires and bumped away along the potholed "road" into this little garden spot. Then he looked back at Moss; maybe seventeen, standing there in dusty sandals, your perfect model of a conscripted teenage killing machine. Moss got the feeling gracious preambles would be wasted. Hoping this was an English-speaking scenario like they said, he walked briskly towards the sentry. "Is the chopper ready to go?"

The guard moved only his lips. Barely them, actually. Had this slight Brit clip, which was kind of funny from a kid looked like he should be jacking cars in Crenshaw. "And you might be, sir?"

"I might be he who they told you to gas that Snake up for."

The guard showed a wisp of smile. He was bored out of his skull, and this looked like a situation he could torment for hours. "I have heard nothing like that, sir."

Moss nodded, understanding all, "Is it gassed and ready to fly?"

"Oh, completely, sir." The muzzle of the carbine moved upwards almost imperceptibly. "But you are, again?"

"I'm the people who gave you your air force in the first place." He looked at himself, a domed reflection in those silver bug eyes. Maybe homey here just likes gunning people down anytime there's nobody around. And this is about as "not around" a place as any, ever.

The guard thought it over. You never knew. But he had a sense about this guy; a foreigner, no tribe, looked like his mean old uncle Tanba. He got the same feeling from that white man behind, as well. "I think I'll just make a phone call, sir."

"Good idea," Moss nodded. "Try Brigadier Mocusta's office."

He got the feeling the eyes behind those little reflecting pools got a little wider. "Please stand easy a moment," the kid said.

Moss took two steps towards the shadow of the Cobra, Doc moving up behind him, but the Guard, moving faster than you'd have thought, had them covered and his domino partners jumped up and grabbed their weapons. Doc stood still, surveying the

14

scene without much enthusiasm. Moss sighed. "Shit, we just want to wait in the shade, homeboy."

"Understandable, sir. But not permitted. Perhaps you could you come with me to the telephone?"

"Aw for Christ sakes."

The phone on the front wall of the Quonset, tall and black with a rotary dial and steel cable to the bulbous bakelite receiver, looked like it should be in the dressing room of some thirties Chicago speakeasy in a Paul Muni film. Moss looked like he wanted to reach through the wires and wring somebody's neck. The guard had been jabbering away in fluid, bouncy African while Moss fumed, but finally got around to telling him what was shakin'. "He says the only helicopter we have is that gunship, sir."

Moss glanced at Hardesty and got a nod. Good, let asshole get in it and fly his hole ass outta here. He told the soldier, "Then I guess we'll have to take the Cobra."

More sonorous yammer into the phone, then he held his hand over the handset and spoke to Moss. "He doesn't think..."

"Listen here, nephew," Moss said with full exasperation out on display. "You tell him if I can't take the chopper, we're gonna come *take the chopper*. Know how I mean that?"

The guard gave him a measured, mirrored look, spoke into the phone, then smirked, "He says to ask for identification."

Moss flashed him a walletful of credentials, said, "Tell him I'm a large, ugly nigger with CIA ID and a shitty attitude."

The soldier chattered into the phone, then turned his mirrorshades to Moss. "He says he remembers you."

SIX

It was a sleepy hamlet, a scatter of huts with no sign of industry. Its location by a bridge across a gorge might have lent it enough strategic value to warrant placing a squad or two there, the U.S. surplus tents surrounding the peaked, round huts on the north side of the town like wedge-shaped green cubs snuggling up to a row of teats. But a training company might have been quartered there by sheer accident, or because some colonel's aunt had a restaurant there. But there seemed to be no reason for either village or encampment. In the melting mid-day, there was very little activity visible, not even in the hammock slung under the shade of a tarp, where a middle-aged black man in olive fatigue shorts and a Barry Manilow T-shirt was sleeping rather noisily. If he had opened his eyes to see what the approaching racket was, and looked past his toes, he would have seen a slight stirring in the ocher dust twenty yards out, like sediment swirling in the bottom of a shaken glass. The dust sifted and heaved, then formed funnels, like fingers pointing to the sky. The funnels swept together, uniting and widening into a focused dust storm, an orb of dust into which a black attack helicopter dropped with a bit of bounce that spoke of less-than-expert handling.

Okay, he did have his eyes open, of course. But barely, registering the big white guy sliding the scuffed canopy back and standing up in the cockpit. Faded chambray shirt with sweat stains at back and sides, khakis that looked like some quartermaster had issued them at some distant time, engineer boots, a wide belt with a holstered automatic pistol. Holding a bottle of Jack Daniels.

Doc made no move to deplane, just looked around what he saw as one more typical nowhere village, currently defended and troubled by an influx of soldiers. He knew there were a lot of people watching him, but couldn't see anybody except the chunky guy in the hammock. Then he saw the dusty, battered "Rat Patrol" rigged Jeep with a bumpersticker reading WE BE BASS FISHIN' AND SHIT and smiled, "This must be the place."

He ostentatiously removed his gunbelt and set it down on the seat, then stepped out. He moved slowly towards the hammock, holding the whiskey in plain view. When he got too close to get back to the gun, the hammock suddenly spun over and he could see the sleeper pointing a smallish machine pistol at him. But also showing him a big, infectious grin. Doc raised his hands shoulder high, one palm out, the other displaying a bottle of Lynchburg, Tennessee's finest. "I'm looking for Major Earl. Do you know him?"

The hammock sentry, who had been called "Sam" ever since he arrived in this outfit due to a slight resemblance to the "Casablanca" pianist, smiled even wider. "Would you mean Jim Dandy?"

"That's him," Doc said. "I'm an old friend of his."

Sam knotted his brow over the implications of that. Finally came up with, "So you're a white man? A soldier? A friend of Jim Dandy?"

Doc nodded to all the questions and Sam smiled wider yet, sticking the pistol inside his floppy shirt and pulling out a huge spliff, apparently rolled in newspaper. "Then you'd likely be interested in this one, friend?"

Doc paused then walked towards him. "Why the hell not?"

Sam grinned around the massive joint as he lit it up, drew it into a crackling glow, and passed it to Doc.

17

Who took a hit, then shrugged and took a much deeper one. Sam laughed and reached for the smoking number. "So you're also a friend of Jim's?" Doc asked him.

"Oh completely," Sam said effusively, smoke leaking from his lips as he spoke. "A highly fine man, Jim Dandy."

"Then you'd probably be interested in this one?" He proffered the bottle, which Sam took in his free hand, miming indecision between two conflicting pleasures, then took a pull of the whiskey.

From behind him, where he'd stood silent as a cat, James Daniel "Jim Dandy" Earl softly said, "I generally like to keep an eye on whatever toxicants move into my troop area."

Doc turned around to take in the most recent version of his old colleague, a large muscular guy around his own age, but looking in better shape at forty-something. Still tight, still beaming at the world out of that boyish face with habitual childlike delight. A happy warrior who had always reminded Doc of Raider stalwart Howie Long. He wore a battered "boonie" hat with an embroidered patch on top showing a marijuana leaf and "100% Use Unit", khaki shorts, jump boots and a loose cotton shirt with obscure unit patches, gold leaves sewn on shoulder tabs, and a pocket tape reading MAJOR DUDE. His blond crewcut was untouched by time, he had the same rebel yell grin, still sounded as SouthMouth as Duane Allman. "Shit fire and save matches. Ol' son gone got ugly on us." He pronounced it "you-gly".

Sam laughed outright at it all and held out the bottle and Jim, who stepped over to take a pull. He wiped his lips on his wrist and gave Doc a very Southern grin.

"So where've you been living?" Doc asked in genuine wonder. "Never-Never Land?"

18

"All part of my rock and roll fantasy, cousin." He spread his arms, putting himself on display. "Rockin' it out keeps a boy young. Now you look at John Fogarty, he looks maybe twenty five."

"Hey, look at John Lennon."

"Now see there? Forever young." He passed the fifth to Doc and reached for Sam's joint. "Long as I don't hang up my rock'n'roll shoes, I'm stardust baby, I'm fuggin' golden."

Doc smiled. He had always smiled a lot when Jim Dandy was around. Everybody did. He passed the bottle to Sam, shook his head at the extended doobie, and said, "We should talk."

"Outstanding," Jim responded heartily. "Let's go requisition some beers. Mocusta recruit you? Thought you'd retired from wasting hoss-tile jungle bunnies."

"So did I." Doc waved at the Cobra. "Want some candy, little boy, hop in my chopper."

"Hey, I'm still a cheap pickup."

"Not all that cheap, actually. They flew me here out of San Tropez to save you from being separated with extreme prejudice."

"Prejudice?" Jimmy Dan was incredulous. "How could they be prejudiced? They're all nigras."

Sam almost laughed himself out of the hammock on that one, waving the bottle and joint to balance himself. "It is completely true, you know. To the very last man of us."

"They've had a change of plans. Or allegiance or something. I flew over them on the road in from Lucumba. They're coming to ask you to resign your commission. With a lot of guns and two Saracens."

Now *that* pissed the Major Dude off. He held up his hands to protest the perfidy of human kind and the military mind. "I ask the assholes for one lousy armored carrier to support my grunts and they tell me they don't have any. But come to fucking me off and it's 'Go see Cal'."

"We might have about a half hour to get out of here. Coming with?"

Shaking his head woefully, Jim bewailed the fortunes of soldiers of fortune. "Another great job down the shitter. We need a union. Collective bargaining."

"At least Vaseline and anesthetic."

Jim grabbed the whiskey, took another deep swig, smacked his lips, and said. "This'll do for painkiller, Cuz."

He blitzed out a quick line of African to Sam, pointing first to the bush, then to a central square with a raised platform at one end. Sam nodded, dismounted from the hammock and scampered off in the indicated direction, but Jim bellowed out in Drill Sarge tones, "Hold onto them horses, there, Sam."

Sam ran back up and grabbed the bottle, handed Jim the smoldering spliff and disappeared towards the tents. Jim toked deeply as he led Doc towards one of the huts.

Inside the cylindrical baked-mud hut, somewhat cooler under the thatched roof, a savagely beautiful African girl in her late teens, wearing a colorful dress that left one taut breast uncovered, sat on a sleeping pallet against the side opposite the short door, hands in her lap. Doc stooped to enter, looking around as he adapted to the shade. There were some nice hides on the floor, a large djembe with goatskin head, low shelves holding bowls and military gear. In the back stood a familiar sight; the flame red Fender

Stratocaster named Nadine, patched into the same little road-worn Pignose amplifier.

The girl didn't seem to notice Jim, but stared intensely at Doc, sitting tense and erect.

"This is Doc," Jim told her. "He's a friend." He nodded towards her. "Doc, Naima."

Naima relaxed, pulling a large automatic pistol out of the dress folds in her lap and laying it aside. She rose gracefully and walked up to face Jim, measuring up pretty well to his over six feet of height, slim and whippy. She looked him in the eyes a long moment, obviously expecting something from him.

"Hey, Naima," he said as leaned in to kiss her forehead, speaking quickly in her native dialect. "I have to leave. So do you. Everything is over. You understand?"

She nodded calmly, still staring into his eyes. "I understand. This is all over."

"You know where to go?"

She smiled, slapped him gently on the forearm. "Of course. To my sister's. In town."

"And to nursing school, right?"

"Nursing school, right."

Jim stepped to the wall and pulled an olive drab canvas duffel bag off a shelf. He pulled out a large roll of funny-colored money and tossed it to her, then starting jamming all his stuff in the bag. It took about thirty seconds. "That should do it, kid. I want you to take care of yourself."

She was putting her own things into a bright green shoulder bag, but turned to laugh. "I have always taken care of myself."

"It's been the best, kid. I'm going to miss you."

"For how long?" She smiled blindingly and tucked the money carefully into her clothes. She picked up the bag, and another one she'd already packed, shot Jim a parting look, and ducked out the door. He zipped the amp into his bag then threw an M-16 with extended magazine over one shoulder and the Stratocaster over the other. They stuck out behind his head like rock and roll wings.

"She was the best one yet, know that?"

"You say that every time."

"And it's always true." He gave a last glance around the hootch to make sure he had everything, then gestured at the door. "Wanna catch my farewell address to the troops?"

"Wouldn't miss it."

"They're the best ever, too."

Doc had bent to the door, but looked back, surprised. "Well, you don't always say that."

Jim motioned him through the door and followed, dragging his duffel bag behind him. "You won't *believe* these guys."

SEVEN

There was a small waist-high platform between the circles of huts and straight lines of pup tents, made of used tires stacked into a square, then filled with packed earth. It faced the open "parade ground" where Doc had landed the gunship. As soon as Jim Dandy jumped up on it, it turned into a stage. The parade space was filled with young African soldiers in newish uniforms, standing in company formation holding their weapons. Weapons in excellent condition, of course, Doc noted from his position standing beside the platform. These kids really did look combat-ready; typical Jim Dandy bivouac and *esprit de corps*.

Jim regarded them with pride and joy, like he'd made them from scratch. Which, Doc figured, wasn't that far from the case. He turned to Doc, passing a munificent hand to commend them to his approval. "The max," he proclaimed. "Magni-fucking-feek."

"I'll take your word for it," Doc said, looking out at the youthful cannon fodder. "They look like all the other colored kids we teach how to get killed."

"Nah," Jim scoffed. "These dudes are special, bro. Check this out."

He stepped to the front of the platform and raised a single clenched fist overhead. The troops clicked to full attention, watching him like sleek black cats. He opened his mouth and ripped out the opening syllables of the old Tokens hit, "Wimoweh".

"Way o way o, ah way oh way oh, umba wim oh way", he sang in a clean, true baritone.

The rows of troops sang back in rousing unison.

"Wimoweh, a wimoweh, a wimoweh, a

wimoweh, a wimoweh."

They repeated the syllables over and over while Jim sang over the top of their harmony.

>*"Near the village, the peaceful village, the lion leaps tonight.*
>
>*Near the village, the peaceful village, the lion leaps tonight."*

The chorus swelled and throbbed from the young throats of the people who invented music, a hundred young warriors fused into a single unit by a master trainer. He cut them off with a chopping gesture and turned to beam at Doc. "See what I mean? These kids are the Kind."

"I gotta admit"

"Remember how there was always the right way, the wrong way and the Army way? Well, around here we got us the Wimo Way." He turned to address the men, shifting into Command Voice. They were fixated on him, faces blank and expectant in the harsh sun.

"We trusted them," Jim Dandy slugged them with his heaviest tones of mastery and reproach, speaking for the ages, "But they are coming here to kill us. You have to learn to live with this shit. You know what to do and where to go. You have about ten minutes to get out of the village--towards the hill."

He let that sink in, caught the eyes of sergeants and natural leaders, then softened his tone, but not the power of his voice. "You are the finest lot of young men I've ever trained and fought with. They can take away your land, they can take your money, and your family. And they might. They can even take away your guns. But they can't take away what you've learned here--that you are warriors, that you can be cheated and killed, but not conquered. You are killers of lions: let them fear you. It's been a pleasure fighting with you."

He paused, centering a silence that grew heavier. He

24

snapped a salute and barked, "Now get the fuck outta my sight before I drop your shit in the sand for a jillion anna half pushups."

The troops broke into a cheer, then a roar, then a soft of chant. He's still got it, Doc was thinking: it's a good thing he never feels like taking over the world. Waved to sudden silence by their Major, the troops stood like knife blades quivering in a tabletop. Then the troop sergeant snapped a monosyllable command and the entire hundred bodies executed a side-facing movement. At another sharp, flat word, they started to march out of view.

"Once in a liiiiiife time," the troop sergeant bellowed melodically. The black centurions sang out in a single raw, beautiful voice over the stomp/shuffle of their own boots. *"The water flowing on down."*

Christ, Doc thought, he's got them doing Talking Heads. David Lynch should be filming this. He watched as the company sang their way past the huts, then broke into a double-time trot, heading for the hills. Jim hopped down from the platform and headed toward the helicopter, swinging his duffel of belongings.. Doc followed, watching the guitar and rifle ride the muscles of his back.

Doc took a look at a suspicious smear of oil on the landing gear while Jim stowed his stuff in the cramped rear seat of the cockpit. He looked around the village for a minute, watching his former command hit the scrub at the foothills and start to disappear, the women and families of the village moving off in another direction with their bundles and carts. Then he hopped flatfooted into the cockpit and stood on the seat. As Doc crawled into the front seat he pulled off his uniform shirt and sailed it off onto the dirt, revealing a writhing array of cut-up muscles. "So what brings you by this neck of the woods, anyway, Doctor?"

"The CIA."

"Holy Hanna, who else? I thought you gave that up."

Doc slid the canopy shut and started running down the switches, pausing where his memory of the complicated dashboards and protocols were hazy. "Here's the tale, Jimbo. Some Cuba Libre locos snatched Jude Mayfield. They're mailing pieces of her to the Company until somebody gets cut loose or I get in and rescue her. Until *we* get in, if you choose to accept."

"Shoulda known there'd be some piece a tail tied to Dragon Rock for you. You still got the hots for that bitch, huh?"

"Whatever I've got it doesn't seem to get any better."

"One thing I like about you, Doc. You're so incurable."

"Hey," Doc had pulled on his headphones, but hadn't started the engine, so he spoke over his shoulder, "She took a teen-aged grunt trying to kill as much of the world as I could before it killed me, and turned me into a photographer. Without her I wouldn't be shooting flowers and fashions and nudes. I'd still be..."

"As big a gun'n'run asshole as me?"

"Hardly as big. I'm aware of my limitations as an asshole."

Doc fired up the 1800 horse turboshaft engine and felt the throb through the airframe. He clicked once and heard Jim in his earphones. "Hard to compete with natural talent. Cuba, huh? On Langley money?"

"That's the picture. No idea what we'll be up against."

"Nice beaches and pussy down there. Good rum and cigars. Pay anything?"

"You're so mercenary."

"Oh, like that's a bad thing,"

The rotors were kicking the sand up, creating an artificial tawny cloud around them, but Doc could see the motion at the bridge. Several skirmishers had run across, checking it out, and waved to a column of infantry behind them. Doc eased it up, the lift-off too wild and wobbly to impress any flight instructors who might have been in the area. Once airborne, the gunship hovered a little shakily as Doc made sure he had it under control. The column had completely enfiladed the bridge and small armored vehicles were approaching the other bridgehead.. Some of the lead soldiers were moving into the village now, and starting to fire.

Jim lent support over the intercom, singing in falsetto,

"Spring little Cobra,
Getting ready to fly
Spring little Cobra,
Spring with alla your might."

The Cobra took a ding, but popped up just as the first Saracen pulled onto the bridge.

As Doc stroked the controls, trying to keep the whirlygig on top and wheels on the bottom, Jim pulled a portable radio from the thigh pocket of his cargo shorts and zipped out the telescoping antenna while studying the advancing troops. "Wanna catch some of the late scores?"

He held the radio up above the sill of the canopy and twisted the dial. Immediately the bridge exploded into a towering, roiling, pillar of fire, plunging both Saracens and several dozen pinwheeling, flaming men into the chasm amid the sounds of screams and automatic weapons fire. Highly surprised, Doc watched the second APC fall, bullets spitting from the gun in its turret. Attaboy, he thought, go down slinging lead.

In his headset, Jim said, "My goodness."

He pushed a tuner button on the little radio and more gouts of flame and smoke erupted from the north side of the huts. The soldiers crouched behind them to fire at the dangerous Cobra were propelled into nothingness with much fanfare. In his phones: "Gracious."

Jim touched a third button and the rest of the huts exploded like the last act of Rambo, wasting many of the three hundred men who had come to make the village and its garrison their bitch.

"Great baaaaalls of fire." Jim slammed the antenna back into the "radio", pocketed it, and kicked back luxuriantly. "Home, little Cobra."

Doc dipped and banked dangerously as he wheeled away from the conflagration that had recently been a human habitation and educational center for violent destruction. As he leveled off he saw the party of women and kids standing on a hillock, staring down at their flaming village. Jimmy knew they'd have plenty of time to make it out, he thought. The man still had it, all right.

He spotted Naima standing slightly apart from the others, tall and feral with her baggage balanced on her head and a small boy on one hip. He pointed and Jim waved, but she was looking at the fire, not the men who had brought it.

"These morons always give us thousands of dollars worth of explosives and then come mess with us," Doc mused as he settled into a flight path.

"Gotta hip these hicks they're friggin' with Mister Gone," Jim drawled, then tore off a wailing blues harp lick, warpily amplified by the intercom.

"So glad you got out of that little jam with your harpoon intact."

"You bet your ass," Jim Dandy retorted, between moaning octave-tongued Little Walter licks. "We might have to make an instrument landing."

On the hill below, Naima turned to watch the chopper, its whocks fading as it moved down the valley. In perfect British accent she softly sang,

"Hush my darling, don't fear my darling
The lion sleeps tonight.
Hush my darling, don't fear my darling
The lion sleeps tonight."

EIGHT

One of several things Moss hated about the Miami airport was that every plane that landed reminded him of the opening sequence of the "Miami Vice" series. And now here come those two haywire jitterbugs, waltzing out of the entry lounge with a bunch of hot chicks around them, just like part of the opener. Probably got unstructured cotton sports coats and pastel shirts and Vuarnets in their checked baggage.

He let Simms deal with them, watching them grab a beat-up "in-country" duffel bag and leather satchel off the carousels. Simms, every inch the gracious pro, shaking hands all around, making nice with that Jim Crow shithead. And the whole time the muzak is coming on with this Miami Sound Machine, Mambo Kings crap. Soundtrack for the show. And here come our guest stars.

Simms matched Doc's stride, polite but not obsequious. "So how was Africa?"

"Well actually," Doc told him, "We were kind of asked to leave."

"See if they get any more of our business," Jim chimed in.

Great, comedians. Moss ignored them, growled, "So shall we get on with this jive?"

Simms looked like he'd just remembered something. "Hey, Herman, it looks like you won't even have to bother with Perez. Why don't you head back to the Embassy and hit the pool." He gave a winning smile, "Get a suntan for a change. I'll take care of the boring part here: just a quick ID and operative briefing."

The air-conditioner wafted a distinct odor of rat to

Moss's sensitive nose. "Why shouldn't I be in on this? Pretty damn important show-up, I'd say."

Simms stopped and looked at him, then at his feet. He spoke with controlled embarrassment. "Okay. It's Perez. You know, he's from Cuba and has a lot of very different cultural attitudes..."

"Does he now?" Moss jumped in belligerently. "One of which is maybe he don't dig niggers?"

"No," Simms said in a flat, loss-cutting tone. "He doesn't."

Moss clouded over like a perfect thunderstorm and opened his mouth to blast, but was interrupted by Jim Dandy, standing on a luggage cart like it was skateboard and opening a miniature airline bottle of Jim Beam. "Well, hell, who does?"

Moss whirled on him aggressively and grabbed his own crotch.

"Your mama's been known to crave some of the juicier parts."

"Well, sure, but who with any class?"

Again, Moss had his response stifled as Simms headed him off and led him just out of earshot for a talk-down. Doc watched, wondering what the hell this whole clown show was all about, but Jim was paying more attention to a Latino kid in white ducks and lime green *guayabera* who left his suitcase under a bench and bopped around to the sounds of *danzon* from the boombox on his shoulder. Moss was gesticulating over there, raising hell while Simms nodded inoffensively. The only words he caught were "banty little racist cocksucker".

Jim swayed with the music, putting a little more in it whenever an attractive woman passed. He was approached by a shady character in Miami Heat T-shirt and raggedy cutoffs who turned out to be selling pirated Dolphins paraphernalia out of his much-

31

patched Hello Kitty bookbag.

Moss was starting to run out of steam and once again sign off on the usual Company bullshit, losing interest as Simms handled and steered him. He half-listened to mission objectives and half-assed rah-rah, eying the two mercenary scumbags they'd scraped up from halfway around the world. Hadda go around our elbow to get to these assholes, and they're prancing around over there like a Vegas act. He watched to see how that Earl cracker would handle being cruised by some religious cultie in an orange robe.

Jimbo had been trying on a Miami Dolphins baseball hat when the mendicant approached him, but immediately switched his interest. Moss watched him inundate the cultie. First time he ever felt sorry for one of the mopes. He was swelling up and intimidating the guy, looming over him like the Tower of Flex and you could tell the gurubait was crapping his robes. Then he started reeling him in with moves and poses that combined circuit preacher, rock star, and siding salesman. Finally he had him under one arm like a mother hen, spieling confidentially, pumping him full of charisma by contact induction. The kid looked totally awed, and now he looked like he'd switched over to a new cult. Snap, that's exactly what it was. Dickhead puts his new Dolphins cap on the kid, who then hands him all the money out of his little begging basket and runs off. Hardesty standing there watching it, just shaking his head, but smiling. Matched set of a-holes.

He followed Simms back over to their recruits, wondering why the hell he'd been pissed off to have to miss going to see that fucking Perez with this pair of deuces. Simms waltzed up to them like a bistro greeter, saying, "Well then, shall we?"

Simms led them out to the hired car, catching Jim

and Doc's eyes to make "cool down" motions and incline his head towards Moss. Luggage in the boot, Moss established in the shotgun position up front, letting those three fools hang in the back seats, he was almost over it all as he reached for the doorknob. Sure, go back to the hotel and goof off, let Simms run these losers. Then four little geeks in orange robes and Dolphins hats run up the car, all bowing and salaaming to Earl. He rolls down the window and they hand him money, he makes some kind of joo-joo sign over their heads and they back away, bent over. Moss slammed the door. Man, this whole gig was starting to suck.

NINE

Doc sized up the Perez mansion with the eye of a man who'd photographed pretentious lifestyle ghettos back before he was making enough money not to. The tasteful front blockhouse with security guards and gates like tank traps had been the first clue, reinforced by the Versailles *porte cochere* and "Old Florida Meets The Strip" attitude of the ostentatious facade, the march through acres of white marble floors and glass soaring ceilingward to better shove Biscayne Bay in your face, the moment of indecision when the squad of bodyguards and friskers wavered between the swooping staircase and brushed steel elevator, the hallways hung with some gallery's fortune in "investments" and the thick doors of carven tropical hardwood. Finally delivered with more menace than respect into a hangar-sized private office that had him casting about for the little plaque announcing it as the work of the designer from "Scarface".

While Perez, a barrel-shaped Cuban whose blocky build and expensive but poorly-inhabited suit were a subtextual billboard for Self-Made Man Immigrated From Nothing; not entirely true. In case his whole manner of slashing a pen on papers proffered by underlings and browbeating his telephone didn't get that across. Doc mentally framed up a couple of devastating shots of the man before he turned his attention to the play of sun on the water outside.

Jimmy was more intrigued by the massive collection of wall ornaments and roamed the non-view-enhanced walls that were lined with glass cabinets and shelves loaded with collections of memorabilia and civic awards. Curious as a kid, he prowled lavishly framed photos of Perez with presidents, Orange Bowl committees and princesses, Jesse Jackson, Jose Feliciano, Don Shula, Dan Marino, Arnold Schwarzenegger, G. Gordon Liddy, Anita Bryant, Don Johnson, and Gloria Estevez. One shot of exceptional interest showed a commando squad obviously heading for Bay of Pigs. Crosses drawn across chests suggested that a much younger but recognizable Perez was one of only two survivors. A shot of Cubans conferring with Kennedy featured a tidy bulls-eye inked over JFK's forehead.

Jim gawked like a tourist at the pictures, awards and gilded attaboys, but suddenly realized that Perez' thick rant was not to some poor bastard on the phone anymore, but directed at Simms. He left the Perez Memorial and moseyed over for a better listen.

Perez was almost spitting his words out. "Cuban-Americans? Refugees? I've lived here forty years and own ninety million dollars of real estate: Am I a 'refugee'?"

He turned to his bodyguards and assistants for disagreement, but found none on their faces. "That bitch Fidel calls us 'gusanos'. That's what we are for leaving our own homes rather than live under communists? Maggots?"

He seemed to be reaching some inner boil-over point. Doc kept an eye out for any foaming or frothing. "Am I a 'Cuban in exile'? How can a traitor exile me from my own country? I am a warrior, fighting a long war for Cuba. Like any soldier, I fight from the field, from wherever I stand."

Jim took in the wall of fame, this street tough risen to highrise and dressed elaborately if to no particular end, enumerating a billionaire's woes to Simms, Doc, and his palace guard. He drawled, "Well, at least you've done right smart since you got up here."

Perez launched out of his high-tech chair, pointing a stubby manicured finger at Jimmy, fuming, "And where is 'up here'? Is this my family's land? Can money buy my pride, my love, my *patria*?"

He waved a disdainful hand at his trophies, dismissing them. "What is this? What is money? The recognition of strangers? Nothing!" He finally hit that psychic tipping point and tore open his coat, whipped a pistol from a sleek Bianchi holster, and started firing at the wall of tribute. His visitors stared in shock as he blasted his keepsakes, showering the room in glass and brass fragments. His staff had apparently seen it before, or worse. He hurled his empty Browning into the shelving and turned on Simms and his crew, rabid and panting.

"Nice shootin', Shane." Jim Dandy offered jovially.

God knows how the civic leader would have received that remark, because the door burst open, spilling three bodyguards into the room, all toting silenced submachine guns. Jim and Doc stood in carefully neutral positions under their cover. Then a slim, alert-looking teenaged boy ran into the room, holding a .9mm pistol in front of him. An intense, delicate boy, he trembled wide-eyed as his gun panned the Americans. Reassured, he lowered it and walked sheepishly to Perez, who regarded him with effulgent pride, but took a scolding tone. "Javier! Have I taught you to run *towards* trouble? Should assassins and kidnappers merely fire guns, so you will gallop right to them?"

Javier lowered his head, but knew he was in no trouble. "Sorry, Papá I thought you were in danger."

Perez wiggled a doting finger at him, then turned him by the shoulder, displaying him to these important spooks. "Gentlemen, my son Javier. As you see, he is foolish and impulsive; running to aid his tough, worthless old father when he should be protecting his bright future, his artist's hands."

Simms was quick off the line, "A brave boy. Pleased to meet you."

Jim Dandy nodded with an approval that the kid just ate up. "Right on time, kiddo."

Perez was glowing as he waved the guards out of the room. His self-destructive ego demon was nowhere in sight as he extended his hand in mock severity. Javier handed over the pistol, which Perez stuck in his belt. Good to have a loaner, Doc thought, I think there are still a few undamaged trophies that might get unruly.

"There was no cause for alarm, son," Perez said fondly. "I was only giving our guests a lesson in relative values." Again he wagged an admonitory finger, "Now back to the studio, no? One doesn't get to Carnegie Hall by running around playing *pistolero*."

Javier smiled, bowed to the Americans, and left, closing the big mahogany doors behind him. Perez immediately turned to them, beside him self in glee at being able to rave about his offspring. "A great pianist! He will be the first Cuban to win the Moscow prize! He lives only for music." Hardening his tone he made his heavy point, "And for his family and country, as you have seen. The finest of young Cuban manhood and he can't set foot in Cuba. Can't play in the *Palacio* in La Habana! Need I explain myself further?"

"That's why we hope to serve you, Señor Perez," Simms said with rich sincerity.

"They prostitute art, rape books, kill God, but above all..." Perez was just getting warmed up. "...they spit on the breasts of music. What is life without these things, gentlemen?"

He spun and bounced over to an un-gutshot cabinet, opening it to reveal hundreds of LP records in plastic protective sheaths. After a short consideration he snatched one out, painstakingly positioned it on an understated German turntable and lowered the high-tech needle. Immediately, hidden speakers immersed the room in sound. "Something to soothe us, Señores? Vivaldi. The Four Seasons."

"Hey, blasts from the past," Jimmy crowed. "Frankie Vivaldi and the Four Seasons." He went into a thin falsetto,

"Walk like a man, sing like a broad,
Walk like a man my soooooon."

Perez stared at him, aghast, and Simms leaped to make nice. "Look, Earl, maybe you'd have more fun walking around the grounds. I know all this formality and longhair music must be boring you."

"Boring? I don't think so. When's the next family values firepower demonstration?" But he headed for the doors with a friendly nod for Perez. "Hell of a stereo, Ace. You oughta pick up some Pink Floyd and rock right off."

Simms, at his elbow and wishing he could give him a bum's rush, hissed in an undertone, "Will you get *out* of here, Earl? These are very cultured people."

"Meanin' they take the dishes out of the sink before they piss in it, right?"

Standing with clenched fists, glaring at this troglodyte *yanqui,* Perez shot out, "What could a man like you appreciate of fine music?"

"Hey," Jimmy said in a tone so heartfelt it could have been taken as a warning, "It's *all* fine."

Perez threw up his hands, looked at Simms for support against Philistines, "What kind of music would a hired killer understand?"

"Grateful Dead?" Jimmy conjectured. "Megadeath? Slayer?"

Simms knew better than to touch him, but was obviously dying to usher him out. "Please, Earl. Wait in the car."

"But firstest and foremostest, the ol' piano-humper his own bad self, Mister Jerry Lee Lewis. The Killer, to y'all." He threw the doors open so hard they bounced back shut behind him.

Simms was immediately all over their host. "I apologize Sr. Perez. I just wanted the men to meet you, thought you might inspire them on this mission."

Perez was openly miffed and suspicious. "Your mission. The one you want to use my valuable, long-term contacts for. Well, I'm not convinced. I don't create networks to waste on a pack of fools."

Simms was not a man to sweat, but he was laboring inside as he stepped up to smother the brushfire that redneck had just set in his most ambitious project.

It wouldn't be hard to get lost in the rambling, hyper-commodious chez Perez, but you could count on the armed retainers to point you right. Jim bopped around the hallways rubbernecking, followed not too surreptitiously by two of the larger bodyguards. He was less impressed by the lavishness than he looked: he'd worked for nigra-rich Latinos before, time or two. He was heading across several acres of white Portico marble towards the inch-thick glass doors deeply sand-blasted with motifs of Old Havana when he heard music. And when Jim Dandy heard music, that's where he went.

The door was ajar and the piano notes were kind of floating out on curlicues, so he nudged it open and got a load. The guards were right on top of him instantly, guns in hand, but anybody could see he was just digging the sounds. The music lounge was a nice blend of lavish and professional, one side with seats where the elect could sit to enjoy, the other side looking like a recording studio with music stands, baffles, sound gear in tidy compartments, and a huge white Steinway grand. Javi Perez sat at the piano, throbbing it with his head thrown back and his eyes closed. Jim and his escort watched him rip a pro level dexterity exercise into a blistering crescendo.

He kept his eyes closed, flexing his extended fingers, until the last note faded to nothing, then opened them to see two of his father's watchdogs standing in the doorway, flanking a guy who looked like Arnold Schwarzenegger, but reminded him more of some fanboy on MTV. "Whoooooooeeeeee," Jim Dandy hooted by way of introduction. "Hot chops, li'l buddy. I mean that's like, Rocket 88. You could be the next Jerry Lee Lewis."

Javi nodded, frowning slightly. "Is that jazz talk?"

"That there's The Rock talking, son." Jimmy bellowed like Foghorn Leghorn. "Lemme, I say, lemme fetch my geetar, we can swap us some licks here."

Javi stared in wonder. "You have a guitar?"

"Never travel without Nadine." Jimmy turned and headed for the outside doors. "Lemme get my ax and we'll jam."

"Help him bring in his instrument," Javi told one of the bodyguards. He looked at the remaining one, puzzled. "Ax? Pig nose? Jam? Do you have any idea what was he talking about?"

"Probably *yanqui* cooking," the muscle told him earnestly. "They'll eat practically anything."

Javi stared at his hands on the keyboards, lifted his fingers up to his eyes. "Do you really think I could be another Jerry Lee Lewis?"

"Absolutely," The guard passed a flat hand in front of his waist to emphasize it. "There's not a doubt."

"So who is Jerry Lee Lewis?"

"He's that guy who wants your change because his kids got multiple psychosis."

They both turned to look as Jimmy came back in with the Stratocaster in one hand and the tiny Pignose amplifier in the other. He chunked the amp onto an expensive music stand, plugged the Strat into the amp and looked at Javier, who was completely dumbfounded. "Lets just take the Pig by the nose shall we, Junior?"

Javier eyed the Fender like a hearse driver looking at a street rod. "Do you have your sheet music?"

In the study so recently the scene of a memento massacre, Simms and Doc had finally been given not only seats in plush modern leather chairs, but drinks. As one of the guards handed a drink to Perez--a Cuba Libre, what else?--Simms was looking content, but not as happy as he felt. "I understand perfectly. Your responsibility to your people who trust you with their lives. And your responsibility to fight for your own son's heritage."

His whole windup and chill-down had been hastily improvised to lead up to bringing the kid back into the foreground, and it worked: Perez brightened visibly, then stood and went over to the stereo system and turned to them as if about to produce a corsage from midair. "Ah, yes, my son's heritage and his future. Would you like to hear something of a young man who will be a giant of the piano?"

Needless to say, that would delight Simms right down to the soles of his Ferragamos. "Of course we would, Señor."

Doc, quite the music buff himself, nodded agreeably. Perez snapped the switch theatrically and the speakers emitted the stately chords of the Nutcracker march,

41

solo piano live.

"Ah, the Nutcracker Overture," Perez proclaimed. "You can see what the Russians were capable of before they went communist."

His smile faded as a ragged guitar line intruded on the piano, leading it into "Nutrocker", neglected classic of oldies radio. He quickly scanned the controls, looked blankly at Simms and Doc without getting back any clues, and ran from the room.

Doc and Simms, along with a pair of guards, were right behind him as he burst through the studio doors into a thundering wall of "Nutrocker". They almost stumbled over three bodyguards, boogieing in place to the driving beat. Javi pounded the keys in a frenzy, leaning forward and violently shaking his pompadour. Jim was leaning back from the waist, his fingers tearing up a patch as they pounded into the final bars.

"What?" Perez shouted, "In the name of the Sacred Virgin are you doing?"

Jim gave the neck of the Strat a quick wipe and said, "Just giving Tchaikovsky the news, Chief." In hushed announcer undertones, he added, "B. Bumble and the Stingers, Rendezvous Records, 1962."

Perez, speechless, searched Doc and Simms for reassurance that anybody was still sane. "What... what *was* that?" he gasped.

"Well, it's got a nice beat and a longhair pedigree and you can dance to it," Doc told him judiciously. "I'd give it a 92."

Perez gawked, so he added, "With a bullet, if you're still in the mood."

Simms was as reproachful as pissed-off. "For Christ's sake, Earl."

"Hey," Jimmy remonstrated, wide-eyed, "What good is a democracy if you can't drag the classics through the mud now and again?"

42

Simms could see it all slipping away again, but was suddenly fired with the inspiration of desperation. He stepped in front of Perez and jabbed a finger at Jimmy Dan. "Look at him, Señor! There is the man we want your Castroite enemies to meet. In a fight to the death."

Perez, regaining his calm under the easy smile of his son, suddenly laughed out loud. He strode across to Jimmy and pounded him ferociously on the back. "To the death! Oh, yes! Oh, you will do wonderfully, one way or the other. Good luck to you, *amigo*. I wish I could see La Habana again myself.

His Strat now slung pegs-down over his shoulder, winding the patch cord around the Pignose, Jimmy nodded affably. "We'll give your regards."

TEN

If Miami provided a splash of Caribe music, hitting Havana was like jumping off the dock into a sea of hip-shaking, foot-shuffling, bootie-bouncing goodjive. The special line for American citizens so they wouldn't get shitlisted for a Cuban visa stamp on their passports wasn't the usual advantage since half of the passengers were Americans; either tourists who got on in Cancun or musicians and journalists heading for the *Sol y Son* festival. Doc was smiling and rhythmically nodding all the way through the line and Jimmy was practically a one-man conga line as he danced in place and jabbered guitar talk to their travel companions.

The good feeling continued as they checked in for credentials at the festival, the lobby of the Hotel Nacionál soaked with recorded, *congero*-powered, brash brass-fired, African-engendered volume. Jim filed through with "Nadine" in a hardshell case he'd picked up in Florida, papered as a member of a band who had never met him before but were getting to like him. Doc, natty in a safari shirt and baseball hat with "Aperture" embroidered across the front, was handed back-stage and all-entry badges by pretty young women at the press tables. Jimmy, more resplendent in a gleaming duck's ass hairdo and Elvisish glamrags, signed autographs for eager fans who had never heard or seen him, Doc walked through greetings from cultural liaison people pleased that he spoke Spanish and delighted to pose for a few flash shots. Altogether a really nice way to arrive in a country, Doc thought as he checked their room's view of the Nacionál while Jimmy sang along with the piped-in *Caribe* music, juggling three bottles of dark rum.

The arrival of Herman Moss was significantly less glamorous. *Can't believe I'm having to be a wetback* into *a third world country*, was his take on it all. *Probably be better than Croatia, though. Maybe. Can't believe I was bitching about being on the Riviera.* As rather dramatically opposed to hiding in the catch hold of a creaking, leaking wooden trawler that would need a months work to quality as a shipwreck. *Catch me ever eating a fish ever again. Even looking one in the eye. Hell, it'll take me awhile to sniff pussy without getting queasy.*

When Chicho, the only Cuban crewman who spoke English--and not really a fisherman--came down to tell him they were about to make the harbor, he checked the all-black scuba suit and tank, grabbed the two waterproof plastic sacks, and went up on deck. The fishermen all looked somewhere else as he got his first look at the lights of *La Habana*, running for mile after mile down the north coast. He zipped the bag with his clothes and the Walkman-style tape player into his matte wetsuit and made sure the other bag was strapped to the tank. It hadn't been one of those voyages that built friendly bonds among passengers and crew, so he took chomped onto his mouthpiece, took a breath to make sure, then unceremoniously tipped over the side.

An hour later he was cursing as he struggled to attach the black nylon line to the slimy buoy so that the bag would hang down below it without fouling in the anchor chain. But cursing quietly, since he was keeping the buoy between himself and a passing Cuban naval vessel. Finally, having arranged the package for easy pickup by passing shitbirds, he found the triangle of blue lights that marked his destination and set out for a long, dark swim. It had been a long time since he swam three miles and took cold comfort in cursing about that.

The lights marked him in to what Simms had briefed him on, a sort of boathouse/godown that looked to have been a rich home before Castro, but seemed to have become some sort of laborers' clubhouse. He'd been bleeding the tank as he approached, so when he shrugged it off and unscrewed the regulator it filled with water and headed for the bottom, carrying his snorkle, mask, and knife with it. As soon as he got his footing and walked toward the rotting dock inside the godown he saw them forming up along the dock, backlit by candles and a kerosene lamp. He cased them as he eased forward and gingerly climbed up the rickety ladder. Bunch of scary damn niggers, was his professional assessment. And every one of them slinging a long machete and showing some stained, degraded teeth. That's it boys, he thought, smile so's I kin see you. He figured out that the ruined teeth were as much a badge of being a cane-cutter as an unsheathed machete carried in hand by the blade. Crushing the pulp to let the sugar run into the mouth is not the sort of practice the American Council on Dental Therapeutics hands out its approval seal for.

God knows what these agri-hicks were doing in an old mansion in Havana, maybe some sort of Socialist R&R. All part of Perez' clandestine network. He sized them up some more as he opened his waterproof bag and removed dry clothes and the Walkman. About a solid 10 on anybody's Don't Rumble With These Motherfuckers list: wiry, fearless, used to hacking the shit out of things all day. But they seemed friendly enough. They sized him up, too, grinning and mimicking him getting dressed, doing what they thought fashion struts would look like. Which Moss thought was funny since they were without doubt the funkiest clothes he'd worn in his life. The crude blended fabric and East Europe cut set off a truly disgusting collection of stains, tears, and fraying. Looked pretty uptown compared to what the Kutter Krew was sporting, though. He realized that he looked like a poor Cuban laborer, which is about and poor and laborious as it gets, and wouldn't draw a second glance if he kept his eyes down and his mouth shut.

He pulled the last item out of his bag and handed it to a cutter who was obviously dying to have something like that. It was a smaller waterproof bag that contained a stack of used, worn twenty dollar bills. At that point he could see all their back molars. He just walked down the line handing each man a bill, then retraced his steps until they were all gone. He had three bills left so he looked at them for their leadership, holding the money up. Sure enough, one of the uglier suckers stepped up, scars on his face as well as the lacerated forearms they all had in common, and nobody objected as he pocketed the extra twenties. He waved an inclusive hand at the crew and mimed drinking, then drunken reeling, and everybody laughed, including Moss. Scarface, continuing in his leadership role, motioned him to follow. As he moved through the ranks of cane-choppin' jungle bunnies, each one grinned and tapped his shoulder. He felt moved by that, but couldn't have told you why. He was off to risk his life on some fool Company scheme, but these guys would just go back to a life of hard physical labor on short rations, dawn to dusk, in drenching, eye-melting heat.

The Kutter King led him up through dank, crumbling stairways into a street-level garage where a bulbous Commie monster truck sat. It could have been Czech or some Tatra cranked out in the gulags, but it had that whole cyberpunk, propaganda poster heaviness to it.

Started right up, though, once he'd crowded in the back, under the tarp with the rest of the canebrake darkies. Somebody had even handed him a machete. He hefted it and they grinned expectantly, so he did some martial arts moves with it, ended up holding it in his teeth. They all clapped and roared in laughter. Come on homeboys, he thought, let's just drive downtown and take over the country, tough shit for anybody stands between. After chugging and farting around Havana seemingly aimlessly, the truck jolted to a stop at dilapidated inn of some sort in the downtown, apparently a rather nice hotel at some earlier point in Cuban history, but currently looking like something out of Dickens. They all waved as he got down from the truck, but were quieter than they'd been since he met them. He stood on the street looking back into the truck bed, and gave them a heartfelt soul power fist salute, then slapped the fist to his heart. They all smiled and made similar gestures, then one of the younger cutters jumped down beside him, carrying a folded piece of paper instead of a machete. He motioned towards the door of the hostel and they went inside as the truck huffed and puffed and blew the scene with its cargo of Socialist Labor Dignity waving silently over the tailgate.

His guide just nodded to the wizened old guy with a Red Sox hat behind the desk, and led Moss through a labyrinth of choked and dirty halls to an equally dirty and dire room. He lit an oil lamp and sat on the bed, unfolding the paper and smoothing it on the rough blanket. It was a map, and he motioned Moss to sit and study it. He laid a caked black finger on the map and said, barely intelligibly, "Is you here."

ELEVEN

It wasn't all that usual to see a big foreigner bopping down the Malecon wearing nothing but baggy swim trunks. But the Malecon has always seen something weirder and Jimmy drew little notice from the nighthawks and beautiful prostitutes of every color from darkest Africa black to pale white and every shade of tan and brown in between. Even the way he was singing oldies as he strode along, smiling at the girls and nodding a happy head at the men.

He hopped lightly over the wall and picked his way down the stone "steps" to the gently pulsing Caribbean. There were boys in loincloths and soggy gray underpants playing in the water, some holding spearguns improvised from inner tubes, old pipe, and straightened fishhooks, two showing fish they'd actually nailed out there to the envy of their amigos. A few *pneumatico* fishermen were coming in, expertly surfing up on the steps in their inner tubes and stepping off to grab their "boats" before the wave receded. A gringo in bright red Blues Brothers surfer jams was a novelty at first, but they got used to it, even to his singing the boobop scat from Frankie Lymon's "Little Bitty Pretty One". He wanted to time this just right, eying the buoy out there in the dusk, its feeble light coming on as the sky darkened. Still enough light to swim out there, and by the time he got back it would be pitch dark. His judgment complete, Jimmy toed the edge of a tier, timed an incoming wave and crouched. His dive was a spectacular display of bunched and released muscles, launching him out to sea so far that he drew applause, which he acknowledged with a wave before stroking out into the afterglow.

It was a long pull out to the buoy against a north shore current, but Jimmy stoked along tirelessly, his brain humming with the same bopping beat: *Oooo, oo oo oo oo oo pa doo.*

He reached the buoy and found Herman's package immediately, released it, and chuffed it down the front of his trunks. He look pretty fat when he got back in, but big-bellied foreigners weren't a rare sight on the Malecón, especially after dark, when the working girls prowled. He pushed off the buoy and headed back in. *Oooo, oo oo oo oo oo pa doo*

He entered the lobby with a Nacionál towel draped around him: a buck U.S. for the kid at the little beer vender cart on the shore side of the Malecón to watch it for him. It was probably not usual for guests to go out swimming at night, but one look at Jim's beamish features would tend to explain any nutso behavior. The clerk nodded politely and handed him his key.

Doc wasn't in the room, so Jimmy just splashed out a hooker of rum and sat down at the table in front of the window to open the case. Inside was a plastic bundle secured with a lot of black duct tape, which he quickly sliced away with his folding Gerber Tactical to reveal an UZI submachine gun without suppressor or folder stock and Doc's sawed-off double-barreled shotgun. Grinning like a kid opening Christmas packages, he took one grip in each hand and held them up for a fond examination. He planted a quick kiss on the muzzle of each, singing softly, "*Little bitty pretty ones, come on and talk to me.*"

Moss, still raggedly dressed in what he thought of as "peon chic", surreptitiously approached a door with a faded sign above it: "Hotel Tañia Guevara". The place, all right. Not as ratty as his bunk the night before, but not short-listed for any Michelin Guide ratings, either. As briefed, he went around to the alley, spotted the rusty drainpipe, looked around and skinned up it to a window that opened as soon as he got to it. He heaved to switch his hands from the pipe to the sill, then cocked his leg to brace a foot on the drain and help push him inside.

He skinned through the window, sort of flopping into the room, and landed on a mattress that had been dragged under it. He thought that was a nice gesture, especially coming from that asshole, Doc Hardesty, who was standing there holding out a hand to help him up. He ignored the hand, rolled to his feet, and looked around the room. Not bad, not bad. Cheap and bare, but clean. Antique-looking table with three chairs. Not that you needed much amenity for staging a raid.

Hardesty reached out to him again, this time with a tumbler of rum. He didn't ignore that.

Hell with those surfer baggies. Jim Dandy jaunted along the Malecón in his usual tropical attire: his dynamic physique clad only in a woven planter's hat, cowboy boots, wrap-around sunglasses, and tight bright red Speedos. And, as usual, he moved through the wondering stares to the beat of his own drum. At the moment, "Speedo" by the Cadillacs on Josie Records, 1956. After a few blocks doing the scat intro, he broke into the lyrics, his whole act drawing smiles as he strutted along singing.

"Well now they often call me Speedo
But my real name is Mister Earl.
And I'm just the kind fellow's
Always takin' other folkses' girls."

He carried a package under his arm, wrapped in gift

paper from the lobby gift shop, and was typically enjoying life to the max. And always singing:

"They often call me Speedo
Cause I don't believe in wastin' time
I've known some pretty women
And I've caused them to change their mind."

He waved at smiling girls, shucked and jived with passers-by, skillfully intercepted a soccer ball from a kids' informal game and headed it into a goal to cheers and waves. As he turned off on a side street he was belting out,

"Some they call me Moe and some they call me Joe
But just remember Speedo
He don't never take it slow."

Three blocks up he turned again, into the front door of the "Hotel Tañia Guevara".

Doc and Moss were sitting at the table listening to some son music on the little old Bakelite RCA radio when Jim burst in, not much going on in the way of conversation. Jim made up for it in sheer effulgence, spieling out his night with two backup singers and his morning stroll. Grabbing a glass and straddling the third chair, he tore open the package; two very personal firearms, a bottle of Havana Club rum, and a box of hand-rolled Partagás Presidentes.

While Doc examined the shotgun and the box of double ought shells held to it with wide rubber bands, Jimmy pulled out a puro and went into the whole ritual of sniffing it, preparing it, and lighting it up. He leaned back, puffing lasciviously at the cigar. "Check this out, Doc. Cuban cigars! I scored 'em right on the Malecón."

"No shit," Moss grumped. "Cuban cigars. They also got Cuban cigarettes. Not to mention Cuban lollypops. Pick up a dog turd, it's a Cuban dog turd."

"Nah, man," Jim drawled, shaking his head at this

lack of erudition. "This is a Cuban Cigar. It's like Beluga Caviar, man. Nam weed. Scotch scotch. It's The Kind."

Moss snorted and Jim smiled slyly. "That mean you don't want one?"

"Damn straight, I want one," Moss growled. "Some of that Cuban Rum, too."

"Then have a little respect."

He handed Moss a cigar with a gentlemanly flourish and splashed three fingers of Havana Club into each glass, along with some imported Coca Cola from one of the bottles he'd snagged in the hotel bar. He took a sip, stole another smoky kiss from the Partagás, and lolled in his chair. "A genuine Cuban cigar and a genuine Cuban Cuba Libre. Does it get any better than this?"

He picked up the UZI and began a pro's sharp-eyed examination. "See now, Herman, you oughta cultivate the acquaintance of white folks. Learn to live a little."

Moss, already pissed off comparing the luxury lifestyle these jackoffs were enjoying while he crawled through grime and pre-emancipation squalor, exploded. "Oh, yeah. This is fat fucking city. My ol' mammy, Lawd bless her soul, always told me if I ate all my collard greens I'd grow up and get to sit around some shithole hotel with a couple of shot-out mercenary assholes in a commie-run slum waiting for somebody to get around to torturing me awhile before they off my black ass, if the jiveass jacking off the machine gun doesn't screw up and waste me first. Oh, this be just kicking ballistic."

Jim shrugged, understanding but unable to accept such a jaundiced view of things. "What else would you do, serve the three trillionth Big Mac for minimal wage? Hell, if I wasn't handicapped by being an overly heterosexual white male, I'd nab one of them agency gigs."

Moss thought it was lucky he was the only one not holding a gun at that moment. He wrestled himself down to an arctic chill, "You're trippin', shitbird. Name me one agency would hire a dog-ass fuckup like you."

Jim glanced innocently at the cigar, rum, and gun, "Alcohol, Tobacco and Firearms?"

Doc laughed at that, but Moss was nowhere close to humor. "Nothing connected to Intelligence, anyway. Fuck this gig and you rabbit-ass mother-fuckers with it."

That caught Doc's interest, and he studied Moss with more interest. Jim picked up on it, too. "Rabbit, huh? Sounds like Herman saw some of Nam himself."

"You don't exactly study for this shit at Harvard."

"So," Doc said slowly, sizing Moss up, "All three of us must have been in about the same graduating class from the Asian War Games."

"Want me to sign your yearbook?" The rum and cigar weren't mellowing Moss at all, maybe making him more truculent.

"Just saying," Doc said. "Maybe wondering why you're laying this big chill-out on us? Have we crossed you in some way?"

"You've been on too many visiting teams, that's what," Moss snarled. He personally thought any American fighting with a foreign army should lose their citizenship, overlooking the fact that he'd been, at one point, an adviser to the armed forces of Viet Nam. "And too many dope runs."

Which made it Doc's turn to look disdainful. "Yeah, I've noticed how the CIA is so opposed to moving drugs.'

"I wouldn't know shit about that. I was five years in DEA, man. Foot soldier in the War on Drugs."

54

"Big whoop," Jimmy Dan said around the tip of his cigar. "Every war I ever been in I was on drugs."

"What I mean. You're always on the wrong side."

"It's been a long time since I was any side other than my own," Doc said quietly.

"Exactly. Which is why you pricks are on my ugly side."

Jimmy leaned over to examine him and said, "You must mean your outside."

Moss glared, then sighed and took a drink. "Ah, fuck you assholes anyway. Here's what's jumpin'. We go to this Ahlvidaydos and meet a social worker: code name Guantanamera."

"That's an easy one to remember," Doc said.

"Really," Jim tossed in. "I suppose if this were Brazil it'd be Ipanema.'

"Who give a shit what he calls himself?" Moss couldn't believe this comedy team. "See can you find out where this Olivaydos place is and we'll hit it tonight."

"They going to let you in?" Jim paused long enough for Moss to cloud up and start to retort, then slipped in, "They might have a dress code."

"So wear a fuckin' dress."

TWELVE

It wasn't that hard to find Los Olvidados if you knew how to pronounce it. But it didn't look all that forgotten: there was a decent flux of locals heading down the decaying street end to the old stone building that would be a lovingly restored historical treasure anywhere but Havana. Not a tourist in the bunch. This was a little harder to get to than the places foreigners sat around sipping Mojitos and looking for Hemingway spoor. All three Americans were somewhat wary as they eased down the alley towards what was sounding more and more like a red-hot music venue. Herman did a double-take as they passed a fading placard on front of another tumbling facade, SOCIALISMO O MUERTE.

"That say, 'Socialism or Death'?" Moss asked, figuring these two would flip him some jive for asking.

"You got it," Jim Dandy said. "Still plaster it all over the place."

"They could use some new slogans, all right," Moss observed. He was getting the impression that if you were a building or superstructure in Cuba, socialism and slow death were basically the same thing.

"They could use some new options," Doc said as they approached the windowless door of Los Olvidados. Its stonework showed some effort to keep it clean, but no real plant maintenance. There was only a small sign identifying the club, but above the door fading letters designated the building itself as HERNADEZ Y CIA. Moss looked dubious. "That's it, right? Olvidaydoes."

"This is your secret contact point?" Jimmy scoffed. "With a big old sign up there saying "Hernadez and

C.I.A." Real covert, there, Herman."

Moss stopped in his tracks, staring up at the sign. "Shit, Hardesty, it doesn't really say that, does it?"

"What part of CIA can't you spell?" Jim asked with full sarcasm dialed on.

"It's just short for 'Compania', Herman. It means 'Hernadez and Company'." He glanced up and chuckled, "That's probably why you guys call it 'The Company', as a matter of fact. Picked it up while you were down jerking Chile around."

"Go ahead," Herman grumbled as he reached the door and examined a rather seedy-looking bouncer who regarded him with overt suspicion and distaste. "Fuck with me, smartass motherjumpers."

Jim pointed to a sign beside the bouncer and laughed. "Must be a class joint," Doc told Herman. "Women have to be wearing appropriate clothing."

"So what's appropriate evening attire for women in a Cuban dive?"

"High heels, knee pads and a light coat of baby oil work for me," Jimmy said as he opened the door to a hot pulse of body heat and an avalanche of tropical dance music.

It was a steamy, jam-packed place straight out of a latter day Hemingway, full of sailors in uniforms of many nations, good time Charlies, women of dubious repute, and a smorgasbord of types that would be considered sinister if they were lounging out in the alley, but here were just more of the happy, boogieing crowd. Alcohol flowed freely and the band poured out a red-hot regional salsa blend that defied you to walk across the room without your hips starting to bounce. Three sailors, evidently Ukrainian, got up and trooped towards the stairway to the wood-railed mezzanine, led astray by two young women with very dark skin, most of it in plain sight.

Three sailors left a table, which the Americans quickly commandeered.

A white-jacketed Waiter took their orders, the exchange shouted over the music, while the guys scoped it out. They peered around after he took off for the bar, taking in the sweltering, smoky darkness and frenetic dancing going on all around them. Most were Havana people who somehow managed to afford a few drinks, Doc figured. With enough offshore money from what few ships hit this port of call to afford to dance like the old days. He looked around the walls at nicotine-yellowed posters: Mamborama, Almendares, Kid Chocolate: there isn't really such a place as the Buena Vista Social Club, though every fourth guy you meet on the streets offers to guide you there. But Los Olvidados filled in very nicely.

He noticed Herman was not just rubbernecking, but searching, so he leaned over to yell in his ear. "You'd think a social worker would stand out in this crowd."

Jimmy stood up and nodded towards the stage. "Well, since it looks like we're in for a wait, I think I'll sit in with the band."

Doc asked, "You know an appropriate tune for a dump in Havana?"

"How about Havana Gila?"

He moved into the crowd, instantly part of the dance, his energetic movement drawing smiles from men and women alike. He reached the bandstand just as one of the three drummers in the nine-piece band launched into an explosive drum solo. He latched on to a guitarist who was taking a break but bobbing to the beat. Doc and Moss watched him point at the guy's ax, do air guitar motions, obviously asking to sit in. Moss thought that was ridiculous, but Doc had seen it happen before.

The guitarist shook his head with the kind of smile we use to ward off crazy people. Jimmy Dan shrugged and reached into his jacket pocket. Moss tensed up, but Jim produced a harmonica, flourished it in front of the incredulous guitarist's eyes, and stepped up to the microphone. He tapped it lightly and leaned in to say, "Breaker, breaker on the Marine Band, good buddy."

Cupping his hands around the Hohner and the mic, he took a deep drag through the reeds, slicing the crowd into silence with a long, screaming blues harp squall. In the ensuing pause, he tormented the harp into the classic 1-4-5 blues riff. Then looked at the crowd with his infectious cracker grin and said, "Little heavy metal fatigue for you, there, amigos and amigettes. Now we gonna bullshit or boogie?"

He lipped the harp again and jolted into a raunchy blues beat that immediately had everybody toe-tapping, grinnin' and spinnin'. The band stared at each other a moment, nonplussed, then one by one plunged happily into the jam. By the last turn-around the guitarist was bending strings like a veteran Blues Bro, laying down an African-influenced Latin blues out of Santana and Bola Sete. The club was going nuts over the novelty and sheer spunk of it all. Jim rared back and loosed an articulated rebel yell. "EeeYeee Haw! So blue! That southern style. Dance the night away."

A buxom waitress shimmied up to the bandstand, breasts lunging around and hands stretched over her head with two slopping glasses of brew. Jim grabbed one, toasted her, took a long deep pull, wiped his mouth with the back of his hand and belched. The guitarist came up and tapped him, offered his instrument with a sweeping bow. Jimmy did a quick tune-up, then stepped up to the mic and told them all, "Now you're really in for it," and slammed into a thudding R&B number. The band, delighted, jumped in with a pronounced Latin inflection. The number quickly wound into a salsa romp, giving way to a wild musical free-for-all. The guitarist had come up with another ax and he and Jim crouched in the classic jam position, bracing into each other while Jim leaned back and flopped his head.

Back at the table, Moss had forgotten about looking around for his secret agent social worker, just stared at Jim's performance. "Damn! The boy do know diddly, don't he?"

"Probably personally."

Moss took a drink, then looked back at the stage. "Man'd be dangerous if he was a nigger."

"I think that's always been his dream, actually."

The jam wound down amid feverish applause and Doc picked up Moss' lighter, snapped it on and held it up like at a rock concert. Just a gesture, but with unforeseen results. A smooth hand the color of unsweetened chocolate appeared from the smoky dark and took his wrist. She steered his hand up to light her cigar, then dropped it and hit him with a set of soul eyes that would have beckoned down the moon.

She moved up until her thighs touched the table. Hard, fulsome thighs, encased in about a foot of red, desperately clinging satin. Above which an ornately fluted midriff led up under a red top that hung loose from a pair of richly resonant breasts, deeply divided by a gold chain with a pendant in the shape of a gold heart with a red enamel Playboy rabbit head. This aggressive, impressive, addressive, cleavage was brushed by long, lank black hair that curved in just enough to provide some framing for a strong, vivid face genetically engendered for the apparent purpose of driving men wild with livid love and lurid lust. Her expression blended an avid embrace of life in all its robust and rambunctious gropings, and a challenging assessment of any man that fell beneath her evaluation. She salaciously sucked smoke from the cigar and cased Doc so searchingly he was glad he'd worn fresh underwear.

"I think she wants to light your fire, Hardesty," Moss said from behind him as he took in the full tawdry splendor of a star of the club, doing business as "Sancha".

"Well, she's certainly welcome to take her best shot."

She turned a simple question into a porn film intro when she said, "Can I sit down?"

"I don't see how," Doc said. "But I'd love to watch you try."

She managed to sit, magnificently, and gave Doc the eye for the split-second it took for the waiter to bring her a drink. She sipped erotically and licked her lips with lascivious promise. "So," she said in a conversational tone, "Who do you guys spy for?"

Doc pointed to the logo on the front of his baseball hat. "Aperture magazine."

"You think so?" she asked, making the arching of her eyebrows a minor sex act in itself. "I think you're imperialist Yanqui spies. I spotted you right off."

Doc smiled and turned to Moss. "Hey, Herman. Says she made us as spies as soon as we walked in."

Moss had handled Jim's musical freak-out and the appearance of Lady Lust, but almost spilled his drink over that one. "Say what?"

"Does it show that bad?" Doc asked her.

"Oh, definitely," she told him, then leaned forward confidentially and spectacularly. "But don't worry, you're OK here, as long as you don't draw attention."

"Says we'll be cool as long we keep a low profile," Doc informed Moss. Both turned to look at Jim on the stage. He'd gotten his shirt off by then, and was laughing his fool head off under a yellow spotlight as he slammed a brace of conga drums with his elbows.

"Don't we just always?" Moss sighed.

The band wound up their current member as Jimmy, who had zoomed in on Sancha from onstage, took a break after much handshaking and backslapping.. He stepped down and walked to the table waving a hero's thanks to the shower of "ole's" and "bravo's". As he came to the table, he gave Sancha a Tex Avery double-take and moved in; dueling hypersexualities approaching pre-critical proximity.

Amenities completed, Jim was taking a deep interest in the new presence at their table. In his usual style. "Listen, Sugarpie. I've got me a major unit here. Play your cards right, you might get some on ya." And remarks of that nature. Possibly because she didn't really understand much of what he said, and also because very little of Jim Dandy's appeal to women was at a verbal level, she rose and headed towards the stairs, a symphony of form following function.

"Whoa!" Jim whistled. "Are them ham hocks, or what? The continental divide, right there. Rump titty, rump titty, rump, rump, rump. Hi, ho, silver tonguin' devil, away."

"Still the butt man's butt man, I see," Doc said.

"Butt head, more like it," Moss threw in.

Sancha stopped and turned her provocative profile to the best angle to launch a blistering look over her shoulder. Jim whistled again, but turned to Doc. "Well, you saw her first."

"You know better than that."

"Oh, yeah, that's right. You get on Jude's scent and you don't even see other women. Well, in that case, excuse me gentlemen. I'm gonna be..." He tightened up into a grit version of limey high notes and sang out,

"Cliiiiiimbing the stairway to heaven."

He headed for the stairs, which Sancha was already ascending; a heavenly and metronomic wonder.

"Junebug figures he's God's gift to women, don't he?"

"Actually, he figures they're God's gift to him."

THIRTEEN

The crib was fairly tacky and not greatly classed up by walls festooned with a variety of posters ranging from Socialist Irrealism to aging sex/glamor to Katholic Kraziness to Santeria All Stars. Not that it needed much décor with Sancha doing a red-hot strip tease under the single ruddy ceiling bulb. Jim Dandy took it in with relish and appropriate audibles, watching her from the ratty bed with his hands behind his head and his trousers tightening up.

This was one "working girl" who didn't disappoint as her professional glad rags came off: the word that came to Jimmy's mind was "revelation". He could have watched her long, strong legs indefinitely, but his interests moved elsewhere as her upper torso slowly and maddeningly came into view. Jehosophat! was his general reaction; show-grade nubbies there, sister. He didn't lose interest when she turned around, either, because what little of her backside was still hidden in the skintight skirt was starting to come out and glow, striking him with the full Havana Moon. He was beyond impressed at that point: more like imprinted. But not so much that he lost all track of mundane concerns.

"Hey, mama," he said when he caught her scorching eye, "Shouldn't we be doing some negotiations up front, here?"

She smiled like a Borgia and leaned to him with upper arms pushing her breasts up and out for him, "Let's talk about boring things later, *chulo*."

"Well," he told her as she crawled tigerishly up the bed and took a proprietary grip on his belt buckle, "I'm way too gallant a cowpoke to haggle with a lady."

That seemed to take care of all financial, and most verbal, distractions for quite a while. Jimmy was far from a stranger to plundering the womenfolk of the third world--and vice versa--but was immediately aware that he was in for something out of the ordinary. And honor-bound to live up to it. She flowed over him, piquing and burnishing, so smoothly that he couldn't have really said when he lost his clothes, just congratulated himself for not wearing underwear. She didn't either, otherwise that striptease might have taken all night.

Any time he thought he had her figured out or nailed down, she would morph into something that drew his gasps or raised his hair. He would melt her down, only to lose his grip as she rose up fierce and muscular as a zoo cat; squeezing out exclamations, drawing blood. He'd be laying back enjoying her maypole dance on top of him, only to have her fall around him like a waif, sliding off him as her eyes alone drew him on top and into the exertion of a man trying to fill a vacuum by sheer sweat and ferocity. He could have sworn she molted, that she exuded warm and fragrant vapor, that sparks flew from her hair and smoke from her ears and rivers of honey from any part of her that touched him. She brought home to him one of his granddaddy's old expressions, "Land O' Goshen!" She was diabolic, demented, a nasty urge, a Biblical plague, a stump-floating flood.

At some point he found himself breathing normally, his brain working, his body nicely sore, his hands laying fondly on firm globes of sun-warmed silk, his vision blocked by a wild tangle of hair, his experience greatly expanded and a-wonder. She flexed her arms, pushed up slowly, her hair falling away like the unveiling of a sculpture. She stared into his eyes awhile then shook her head and tapped him twice on the chest. Then reached to the rickety table beside the bed to grab him a cigar. She popped it into his mouth and lit it, then moved her delectable torso erect to stare down at him. All without ejecting him from their primal connection, or completely stopping the communicative contractions and squeezes that kept him from any belittling tendencies.

Jimmy took a long draw on the Cohiba panatella and blew out a long, satisfied spume of fragrant smoke. "Hot damn, pussycat. That was about honey in the horn. A bargain at any price."

Sancha still toyed with him languorously, cutting her eyes sideways at him as she murmured, "Any price? How about that million in aid to Perez? Or those tank rockets to Punta Sur you promised the last Cuban you fucked?"

Jim regarded her for a long beat. "Know what, sugarbuns? I don't think I caught your name."

Sancha grinned wickedly. "About all you didn't catch."

He winced. "Damn. You mean more than that smile is infectious?"

"Just teasing, you, lover-man. My friends call me Sancha. But you can call me Guantanamera. At your service."

"*You're* the social worker?

"Can you think of any work more social than this?"

Jim ceded that with a shrug and flicked his ash into a tin ashtray shaped like a 1950 Chevy convertible. "So why 'Guantanamera'?"

Sancha yawned and leaned forward, her swollen mahogany nipples descending regally towards his lips. "Cause I'm from Guantanamo. Duh."

Jimmy figured there were better things to do with

his mouth than talk at that point, but just had to say, "Politics should make bedfellows, not the other way around."

Sancha sipped demurely at a double Cuba Libre as Jim clued his comrades in on some of the less expected developments of his dalliance upstairs.

"She wanted five million and a battleship, but I broke her down with sheer sexual animalosity."

"Actually, I think they already paid Perez," Moss said dismissively. "Anyways, nothing to do with us."

"How about the rockets?" Doc asked, out of idle curiosity.

"Shit, why not? We Be War Toys. Does this mean she's hooking us up with locations and logistics?"

"Yep," Jimmy drawled. "Only on condition that I keep hosing her down. There's espionage advantages to being a hunka hunka hunk..."

"Your head wasn't so far up your ass," Moss interrupted the Elvis homage, "You wouldn't get that echo."

Sancha abruptly stood, leaned over to treat the guys to a spectacular cleavage shot while giving Jim a thermonuclear kiss, then shimmied away. "*Hasta mañana guapos.*"

The men watched her saunter off, then looked at each other. Whew.

"So this Calavera guy she's talking about is Cuban?" Moss asked Doc. Try getting a straight answer from that other dickhead.

"Hard to say. It means a skull, so it's probably a nickname, could be anybody."

Moss nodded, drained his glass, and stood up. "We better split. We'll meet her tomorrow and lay the thing out."

"Aw, I wanted to sit in on a few more jams."

"Didn't she say we should kind of minimize our presence here?"

"She wants a guy to minimize, she's wearing the wrong dress."

The doorman solemnly shook each of their hands as they left, giving each a farewell nod.

To Doc, he smiled slightly. *"Mucho gusto, yanqui. Gracias y adios."*

With less warmth, he told Moss, *"Buenas noches, Negrito."*

He was obviously sorry to see Jim Dandy leave, and pressed his hand in both of his own. *"Que te vaya bien, Señor."*

As they moved towards the corner, where a 1952 Ford Meteor Customline with "Taxi" stenciled on its door awaited them, Moss groused, "How come we're "Yankee" and "Negro" and you're "Señor"?"

"Pretty obvious, I reckon," Jimmy said as he sped up a little to claim the "shotgun" seat in the classic. "I got señority."

FOURTEEN

The snorkles sliced through black water, one of them burbling the theme from "Jaws". But fell silent as they approached the dock, veering into the shadow that the boathouse cast in the light from the well-lighted Bautista-era mansion set back among palms and a bougainvillea-covered fence.

The three breathing tubes slipped under the dock, then rose in the water, hoisted by the goggled heads of Moss, Jimmy, and Doc. All three looked around in the dim light and cocked their ears for the footsteps of the lone sentry pacing the old boards of the dock.

The lookout, a big Slavic blond, stopped at the end of the dock, his AK-47 dangling while he rolled a cigarette. He was about to strike a light for it when Jim Dandy exploded out of the water behind him, vaulting onto the planks by sheer upper body strength. Before the sentry could react, Jim sunk a choke hold on him and stripped his rifle away with his other hand.

Doc and Moss popped out of the water and muscled up onto the dock, rolling to swing their legs up and come smoothly to their feet. Doc grabbed the AK from Jim, sticking his shotgun into his waist. Moss faded silently away towards the house.

Doc moved up close to Jim and spoke very low. "Does he know where Jude is?"

"Les jus' find out," he answered in the same undertone. He spoke directly into the lookout's ear. "Where's the woman, Hoss? *Donde está la gringa?*"

He carefully loosened his choke hold and the watchman gasped. Mindful of Jimmy's powerful forearm on his throat, he spoke quietly in a strong

Slavic accent. "I don't know about woman."

"That won't do," Doc said in a slow careful delivery, more for the lookout's ears than Jimmy's. "If he doesn't tell us, kill him."

Bumping his arm against the stressed Adam's apple, Jim muttered, "No rush, I hope."

He spun the lookout to face him, but there was no chance to cry out before he had both hands on his throat. He swung the man's feet over the side of the pier, holding him suspended with no apparent effort, then slowly knelt to lower him into the water for questioning.

The lookout showed fear as he sunk into the water, stared into the implacable face of this hulking monster who handled him like a child. "No, no! I don't know swimming."

"Good," Jimmy told him quietly. "Then this won't take so damn long. I've got me a hot date."

Desperate, but smart enough to keep his voice down with Jim's thumbs on his windpipe, the sentry gasped, "There is nothing. I know nothing."

"Well then," Jim drawled, "We got us some time to know swimming."

He released the sentinel, who immediately started floundering, just out of reach of the dock. Jim stood and started doing "The Swim", moving his hands in an exaggerated crawl motion, then holding his nose and shimmying down as though sinking. In a low baritone, he sang, ala Bobby Darin.

"Well, just keep... splishin' and a splashin'
Movin' and a groovin'"

The lookout was having major trouble by then, taking in water. Jim sang on.

"Thinkin' that you're sinkin'"

The lookout was getting desperate as Jim crouched

over him warningly and sang with heavy insinuation.

"Dyin' if you're lyin'."

Between gasps that were getting as much salt water into his mouth as air, the big Slav pleaded, "Please, I am telling everything."

"Bout time," Jimmy said acerbically. "Inquiring minds wanna know."

He reached out to grab the drowning man by the shoulder of his tunic, holding him on the balance between safety and slipping back down to what he was seeing as the proverbial watery grave. "Speak right up, old son. Don't be backward about being forward, now."

"No women. No women," the sentry gasped. "Only Calavera and Janko."

"No more guards?"

"Two. At the front."

"Not bad for your first lesson," Jimmy beamed approvingly. He pulled him onto the dock. "Maybe we'll get Sancha down here to teach ya breast stroke."

The guard looked confused for the thirty seconds it took for Jim to choke him unconscious. Pulling a roll of duct tape from inside his waistband, he taped his mouth, then whipped it around his hands and feet. Standing, he raised his hands like a calf roper, signaling time.

"See how Moss is doing out front," Doc said, checking the AK. "I'm going through those glass doors on the patio there. Try a side window. Three minutes or until I hear shots. If you hear any fire or windows breaking, come on down."

"Sounds good to me. If that doesn't get it, run Hail Mary out the shotgun."

Moving down the dock, Doc said, "Sounds like a cardinal sin."

"Only sin the Cardinals did," Jim Dandy sneered,

"Was move to a numbnuts burg like Phoenix and stick Saint Lou with them dogass Rams."

FIFTEEN

Doc bellied up to wall, peering through big French doors into a luxurious, tasteless living room. The sterile Las Vegas lobby effect was not so much spoiled as distracted by a serious set of free weights and a collection of punching bags and martial arts gear in one corner.

The obvious owner/operator of the physical culture paraphernalia was the big, muscled blonde hunk who posed in front of a full length, beveled-edge mirror admiring the way he pulled off a series of biceps curls (like he needed them). He wore only karate pants, Kung Fu shoes, and a sheen of golden sweat. He pumped his big boy iron to the beat of loud, brutal hip-hop from a German boombox placed on a hardwood sideboard. The "music" encouraged Doc to slide out a surreptitious hand to try the doors, which were locked. He immediately produced a nasty-looking knife and slipped it between the doors, divining the lock. He froze as Jim Dandy slid into the lounge from a side door, moving towards Mr. Hypertrophy with an exaggerated tippy-toe that Elmer Fudd would have found ridiculous.

Doc watched him with a faint smile and when Jim was almost on top of the hulk, tapped lightly on the glass. The muscleman turned without missing a beat of the dueling dumbbells, frowning expectantly. Jim pounced on his exposed back like a cat, sinking a quick headlock and screwing an UZI into his ear. He met the lifter's spasm of resistance with equal force, then nudged his hip to take him up on his toes and prevent any use of his legs and trunk. Speaking conversationally, he announced, "Avon calling."

Doc flipped the bolt and moved into the room, covering it with his sawed-off. He slid along the wall to the main door and moved cautiously through into a darkened hallway.

Jim walked the hunk over to a straight chair and nudged it sharply into the backs of his knees, sitting him down abruptly. He had his tape out instantly, strapping him to the chair, then winding three quick pulls around his mouth and face before releasing the headlock. He tousled the damp blonde hair just as Doc came back in, followed by Moss carrying two more AK-47's. Jimmy glanced at Doc, who shrugged. "Nobody home."

"Cept two guards currently tied up in the lily bed," Moss amended.

Turning back to the straining weight freak, Jimmy crossed his arms on his chest and said, "Time for Twenty Questions, huh?"

"Let's get straight to the buzzer round," Doc said tersely. He crossed to the chair and snatched the tape off the mouth of the prisoner, who cursed in Slavic gutturals.

Doc slapped his hand over his mouth, hard, and said, "Where's Jude? The woman whose finger you cut off?"

He removed his hand, awaiting information, but the novelty of that remark stopped the Slav. He stared back and forth between the three men, as if questioning their sanity.

"Woman?" he blurted in a thick formerly Soviet accent. "Finger? There is no woman here. We despise women. You leave. Now."

"You're not clear on the concept, kid," Doc rapped out in a tough and forbidding tone. "If you don't tell us, we're going to hurt you. Or worse."

"You mean torture?"

"Well, duh?" Jimmy drawled. "You got a problem with that?"

The captive stared at him, obviously still smarting over a huge mound of hostile musculature like himself being so easily taken down. "What kind of animal are you?"

"Rock 'n'roll animal to you, Solopecks. I'm Jim Dandy and I'll be your torturer tonight. Our daily specials are fire, electricity, and some nice maiming, but I can't recommend the sexual degradation."

"You are crazy." And from his point of view, that wasn't so far-fetched. "Do you know where you are?"

Doc ignored the question, having spotted an electric chafing dish on the sideboard. He stepped over to unplug the hotplate and show it to Jimmy.

"Excellent choice, Brother Hardesty. Preparation right at your own table."

Doc flicked his knife out again, slashed the karate pants down the sides, and jerked them out from under his ass. He pricked the hard glutes with it sharply, causing them to levitate off the chair. He jammed the hotplate under them and taped their owner down onto it. You could tell he didn't care for the situation.

"What in hell is this?"

"Desktop torturing." Jim pointed, helpfully, "Be sure you get full contact with the hanging tender, there, Doc."

The light was dawning on their subject and he frantically yelled, "Nothing! Absolom is not even here!"

Doc froze in shock. Almost in a whisper he said, "Absolom?"

Moss was just as stunned. "Oh, no, man. Oh, holeeeeee shit."

"I think it's finally starting to focus up. And I don't

like the picture."

"It's gotta be the guy," Moss was nodding, stricken. "Absolom fuckin' Muto."

Jimmy looked at them both, then grabbed the weightlifter's lower face in a steel grip, squeezing his mouth grotesquely. "Talk to me,muthafucka!"

"Hey, listen, what's your name?" Moss asked, urgently.

Slurring through Jimmy's grip, his reply was, "Whine choo fuck off?"

"Whynchufuckov?" Jimmy asked brightly. "Sounds Russian."

"Close enough. He's a Serb. Aren't you Janko?" The lifter glowered silently, but Moss nodded affirmatively. "Janko Hzovel. He's been running with Muto since that Bosnian clusterfuck."

Doc frowned, trying to add it up. "Why would they turn up in Cuba?"

Tearing his jaw from Jim Dandy's grasp, Janko shouted, "Because everywhere else they sell out to capitalism: here they still try having revolution."

"Socialism or Death."

"Exactly." Janko nodded.

Doc leaned back on his heels and gave Moss a long look. "Lets take a little truth break here, Herman."

"Long overdue," Jimmy said. "Meanwhile, I'll warm up the bullpen."

He dragged the chair to the sideboard, plugged the hotplate into its extension cord, and turned to regard Moss with arms folded severely. Doc was also giving him a very hard look, which was defiantly returned.

"Absolom Muto, huh? Isn't he sort of the current Carlos the Jackal?"

Moss gave a bitter laugh. "Shit, those Jackal types

get the headlines because they kill a few people in an airport. This cat kills off whole countries. He's masterminded some fiendish shit. He talked Hussein into the Kuwait thing. Helped set up their germ warfare action and split with him because he didn't use it on our troops. Had a lot to do with Korea and Pakistan getting nuke programs. Damn near pulled off having the Zulus and Mandela's bunch massacre each other. He might even *be* a Zulu. He hates whites and wants 'em all dead."

"Hell, he should try Louisiana."

"Amen to that," Moss said with feeling. "Meanwhile, what he's up to now is a deal for the Latin America countries to stop paying foreign debt all at once. We've got tapes of him talking to Danny Ortega. He figured out the Sandanistas should allow that election, so the heat would come off them for awhile."

"Sounds like a CIA dream come true," Jimmy chuckled. "Sure he doesn't work for you guys?"

Moss scowled. "True story, dickhead. Homey here is like public enemy number one, worldwide. How you like it now?"

"Not much," Doc muttered darkly. "Thanks for letting us know about all these little details."

"Word, man," Moss said to him seriously. "I didn't know who it was 'til just this minute."

"Well, if you can't take the word of a CIA agent..." Jimmy chimed in.

"I don't give a shit what you believe, you peckerwood prick," Moss snapped.

"I'd sooner believe Mister SuperCuts here," Jim said. "Especially after that hotplate hots up a little more."

"Think of it as credibility enhancement," Doc said as Janko started cursing again; a good indication that his hotseat was getting hotter by the minute.

Jim slapped the tape back over his mouth and gave him the eye. "Think of any answers yet?"

Sweating with the pain of the relentlessly increasingly ass-burn, Janko nevertheless shook his head.

"That's cool," Jimmy idly commented. "I don't believe people until they're smoking anyway."

"Don't you think this kid is kind of young to smoke?" Doc was looking down at Janko with a cruel detachment.

"Kind of young to be the jiz jar for some international asshole, too."

Janko was twitching and grimacing at that point, his rectal temperature getting up towards Roast.

Moss gave a sour frown. "You guys are really getting your grins outta this shit, aren't you?"

Doc stepped away and beckoned Moss to follow him. Jim stepped over as well, conferring too low for Janko to hear them.

"I don't like seeing anything in pain," Doc said flatly. "I think it's sickening you guys do things like this for a living."

"But you do what it takes, right?" Jimmy put in.

"That's it," Doc went on. "I'd rather give him all-weather tread on his ass than get any more fingers in the   mail."
"Sorry if we're not as subtle and socially conscious as you bleeding hearts up at Langley.

"We do what we have to do, too," Moss said, obviously getting totally pissed. "We just don't make it a comedy special."

"Could have fooled me," Jim snickered. "Some new material and a little work on your timing , you'd be as funny as the ATF. You know what they say: Laugh and the world laughs with you, cry and you're a pussy."

"And perceived pussies get fewer confessions. You don't like our act, bring some truth serum next time."

Jimmy brightened. "Outstanding idea. How about dexamils and XTC while you're at it?"

"Meanwhile," Doc said with enough intensity to stop Moss from any remonstrations. "Get into the Mutt and Jeff, here. If we can scare him into talking it'll actually save him some pain and us some damned time."

Moss glared at him, then nodded. He turned and walked over to Janko, who looked up at him with a last shred of hope, his hips straining away from the red hot element, his face pouring sweat. Moss gave him a hard stare, his face a stony mask, then spoke in a sarcastic ghetto cackle. "Aw right. Yoouuung blood. Skintight, white, and up outasite. Yawl leave me something, hear?"

Janko's face collapsed and he slumped, no longer trying to escape the burning.

"All we want is the woman," Doc said in a neutral tone. "Tell us where she is and you'll be okay."

Janko nodded his head frantically.

"Okay," Jimmy told him in a cautionary tone. "But we gotta buy it or we're not speaking to you until you're branded, maverick." He snatched off the tape.

"Nothing!" Janko screamed. "Kill me! He's not here! There is no woman. No woman, you understand?".

Jimmy did a hook shot, sinking the wad of tape in a trashcan across the room. "Fuck this noise. If there's no women around, let's set the explosives, throw the chili out the window and let the dadburn shack burn down. C'mon, I'm hornier'n a two-peckered billygoat and I think it's curable."

It took Janko a second to sort that out, but got the picture. "No! You would not doing that!"

Jimmy raised his eyebrows, sincerely confused. "What the hell gives you that idea?" He pulled a length of wire out of his waistband and started patting his pockets. "Where are those goddam blasting caps? Well, I'll find 'em time you guys bring up the dynamite.

Janko, horrified, yelled, "No! I am tell you. Stop!"

Doc cut the tape and yanked the hotplate from under his butt. Janko slumped, sobbing.

"So tell," Doc said.

Janko shuddered in a deep breath and pointed upward with his chin. "Upstairs. Don't hurt him, please."

Doc hacked through the tape and wire, hauled Janko erect by his hair and marched him towards the door, sawed-off in hand. Jim and Moss, weapons ready, followed him.

"God, *I* was afraid he wouldn't talk," Moss said.

"So was he," Doc answered him. "That's how it works."

"But he's so dug in on enduring pain," Jimmy explained cheerfully, "That he didn't think bluff when I swung to blowing the building. Whiffed him on a change-up."

"Educational." Moss shook his head and pursed his lips distastefully. "You guys are like Beyond the Valley of Good Cop/Bad Cop. God forbid I ever fall in the clutches of assholes like you."

It hit him as he started up the stairs. "Aw, shit! I already did."

SIXTEEN

"Must be, like, the war room," Moss mused, staring around the upstairs office space. There were charts in several languages on the walls--along with pictures of Che, Ho, Idi Amin--and four computers on tables set around the walls. A central table was littered with folders, cups, and ashtrays.

He and Jim both cased the place carefully, weapons ready. Doc half-dragged Janko into the room, surly and obviously ready to pull something desperate.

They'd cleared the room quickly on their first search, and missed a few things. Jimmy pointed to a faint stain left by a spilled coffee cup, his finger tracking it towards a wall-mounted printer console. He squatted and looked closer. In his best Fudd impression he blubbered, "I'm huntin' tewwowists, huhuhuhuhuh."

He duck-walked towards the console, noting where the dim trace of a heel print was cut off by the bottom of the housing. . "Wook, tewwowist twacks." He touched the barrel of his gun to his lips and stared around the room. "Be vewy vewy quiet."

Doc didn't get into the spirit of play. "Open it."

Janko, devasted, pleaded piteously, "Please..."

"Okay," Jimmy said in exasperation, "*Please* open it. Jeez."

Janko pouted and Jim swung around pointing both his UZI and the AK at the wall in a two-gun *pistolero* pose. Janko, at the point of tears, shambled to the wall and pushed a hidden lever that allowed the console and a section of wall to swing out, revealing a small hideout behind it.

All three Americans had maximum firepower trained

on the little cell, which contained a five-gallon plastic water jug, a chemical toilet, and Absolom Muto, sitting on the porta-john with his pants around his ankles.

Doc scanned Muto closely. He would have made an interesting photo study. A slightly built black man in his fifties with gold wire glasses on a plain, strong face that could have belonged to Desmond Tutu if not for the unmistakable stamp of much pain, evil, and cynicism.

Jimmy relaxed his vigilance and nodded in a neighborly way. "Been sitting there all this time?"

Absolom nodded easily. "I've been a little constipated."

"No shit?"

"As you say."

Suddenly Janko snatched a box knife off the desk and brandished it, backing towards the door. Jim poised to pounce on him, Doc worked his free hand towards the pistol at the small of his back.

"I am sorry," Janko wailed. "I love you! Goodbye!" He jabbed the knife into the side of his own throat, powered by full discharge of his powerful arms. Blood gushed from his severed neck and he fell over, dead almost instantly. He hit the central table, spun face up, and lay there seeping a red pool.

Absolom looked at the body and shuddered. "What a sickening waste. And I did love that boy." He pondered his loss for a long, silent moment then turned to Doc without changing expression. "What do we do now?

"You tell us where the woman is. June Mayfield. Right now."

"I would." Absolom said with obvious sincerity. "But I have absolutely no idea what you are talking about."

Doc looked at him while he sat, at ease even though

bare-assed in front of armed enemies. He glanced at Moss and said, "I think he's telling the truth."

"Bout the only one, I'd say," Jim Dandy added.

"Of course I am. I have no stamina for torture. I want only a clean death without pain."

"But you never cared how many other people die in agony, did you?"

"Not at all," the super-terrorist replied candidly. "In fact, I wouldn't care if everyone died. Is that strange? That poor boy was the last thing I loved in this life. Now I have nothing but cold hate, and it's not enough to make me care one way or the other."

"Aw, man," Jimmy commiserated. "Sorry about your buttboy. We weren't out to kill him, or nothing."

"No," Muto agreed. "Just to kill me. And anyone that got in the way, of course."

"Well, no," Doc said firmly. "We weren't. We just want the woman."

Absolom spread his hands, as if demonstrating their emptiness. "There is no woman. Perhaps they told you this woman was here in order to inspire you to kill me."

"That about the picture, Herman?"

"Starting to look that way."

"We'll have to have a little chat about that later. For now, let's just throw this poor bastard back and get the hell out of here."

Moss paused uncomfortably, then focused on a wall chart as he muttered, "Well, see... "

Jimmy laughed. "You got a hit out on him, huh?"

"Looks that way. You see how they've been telling me every little thing about this fuckin' fiasco. Standing hit. Absolom here ain't just some po' harmless little homeboy. He's a monster. Very dangerous to American interests."

Doc wasn't feeling all that happy with Moss and company at that point. "Don't you mean us white boys' interests?"

Moss snorted. "Yeah. I should probably let him recruit me, huh?"

"Well I'm telling you right now for certain, cousin. I didn't sign on for this shit."

"Not this particular flavor of shit, anyway. You want him dead, you kill him. I'm not in that line of work anymore."

Moss looked at them, then at Absolom, regarding them incuriously. "So I get to be executioner, huh?"

"It's a bitch when you can't chump somebody else into the dirty work," Doc said bitterly.

Jimmy squatted to look Absolom in the eye. "Couldn't you try to escape or something?"

He gave a semblance of a smile and said, "But I've already escaped. One of you will be man enough to kill me. Since none of you will be man enough to let me go."

"So you won't promise to never, ever do it again?"

Moss touched Jim's shoulder and he stood up and stepped back. "You're saying you're ready to die?"

"Oh yes. For a very long time."

Moss nodded, "Solid, man." He swung his confiscated AK up and put a single shot through Absolom's forehead, blasting him back into the hideout in a shower of gore. He bent to stare at the body, then straightened up and looked upwards. "*Fuck* this gig!"

Jim stepped over to him and laid a hand on his shoulder. "It's just the damn job, man. Don't mean shit."

Moss whirled out from under his hand, rounding on him with the rifle pointed. "I know what it means, you whitebread motherfucker. It means keep your cracker-ass hands off me."

Calmly, Jimmy advised, "Do be cool, cousin."

"Don't do that shit, Herman," Doc said placatingly. "Just chill out and we'll go home."

Still pissed, Moss snapped, "Why should I baby this asshole?"

"Cause sooner or later," Jimmy said, with the air of a patient teacher, "You have to blink."

Moss brandished the AK in his face. "So what if I do, fuckhead?"

"Weeeeell," Jimmy deepdish drawled. "The sooner you do..."

Moving too fast to be clearly seen, he snatched the gun our of Moss' hands, reversing it and dropping out the magazine in a blur of motion. "...then the later it's gonna be."

Moss stared at his hand, then at Jim, who was twirling the assault rifle like a gunslinger's pistol. "Guns are over-rated as equalizers," he lectured lightly. "I mean, you're still who you are."

Moss had recovered his aplomb, and also his piss-off. "And who the fuck are you?"

"Me?" Jim Dandy asked incredulously, not believing such ignorance of the obvious. "I'm the guy who put the bomp in the bomp shoo bomp shoo bomp, not to mention the hot dang in the rang a dang a ding dong. I'm the queekest straw in the third world, Babalu. Wanna not see it again?"

Moss clenched his fists at his side and stared upwards like a suffering prophet. "Fuck this gig with a long and limber dick."

Jimmy snapped his fingers. "Hey, that reminds me. My date. Let's head it back to town."

As he spoke, a side window shattered, blasting glass throughout the room. Immediately a single shot sounded.

All three men hit the floor as a burst of automatic fire raked the walls above them. Jim rolled over and shot out the overhead lights with his UZI, but immediately a searchlight blazed through the broken window, making Frankenstein shadows.

An amplified voice boomed out, ringing with no-nonsense Spanish. *"Atención en la casa. Sabemos quienes son. Somos dos cientos soldados, bien armados. Estan arinconados. Rindese si quieren vivir. Tienen cinco minutos antes que les fusilamos."*

"Sounds like we're fucked," Doc said, tucking away his shotgun and checking the receiver of his AK.

"My Spanish must be improving," Moss snarked. "I figured that out."

"Hear them tell it," Jimmy said, rolling over under the window. "Let's take a little peek at these bigmouths." He popped up and down quickly and said, "He was right about 200 guys, I'd say. Definitely well-armed. What you figure they're selling?"

Doc cupped his hands to his mouth and rose up to call out, but flattened again as a sleet of bullets took out the rest of the window and most of the charts on the opposite wall. From the floor he asked, "How do you communicate with people who just won't listen?"

Jim shot the bolt on the sentry's AK and said, "Body language." He yelled out the window in a James Cagney snarl, "Come and get me, coppers."

After the answering shower of bullets died out he looked at Moss and Doc. "Well, we got up the gumption to go gunfuck these geeks or not?"

"Cut it out, Earl," Moss snarled. "Didn't you ever see Butch Cassidy? "

"Bout twenty times. But why don't they ever show what they did after they escaped?"

"Knock it off, Jim," Doc said wearily.

"The one to see is The Wild Bunch," Jim continued with a film-fan's enthusiasm. "They got some beaner-ass army up to their ass and they blow em away and bail. So, are we not men?"

Doc sighed. "Have you got a white flag?"

Grinning, Jim snapped out a handkerchief. "Never leave home without it."

Moss glared. "I was afraid we'd have to waste you ourselves."

Jimmy gave an admonishing shake of his head. "Their union might object. We're in enough trouble."

"We'd better hide the bodies first," Doc said, crawling towards Janko's bleeding corpse.

Jimmy nodded. "Neatness counts, even in terrorism."

Doc and Moss stayed as low as possible while wrestling Janko's body into the chamber beside Absolom's. Jimmy used a wad of printer paper and Absolom's trousers to wipe the blood from the floor. "It's better they don't find any of this," Doc was explaining. "Don't give them anything to go on, don't piss them off any more than we already have."

"Hey Herman, best you slip in there, too," Jimmy added as he stuffed the blood-soaked wads inside. "Sit tight, see can you slip out and see about some help. And when you can come out, lose them bodies, and I mean good."

"Why me?" Moss was understandably suspicious.

"You're the only one the guards never saw," Doc said. "And maybe the best one to try to call the cavalry or at least report us missing."

Moss could see it, but what he said was, "Shit."

He edged into the bolt hole, looked around and sat on the toilet. Doc started edging the wall back into position, but Jimmy popped his head in and grinned. "Oh, and Herman..."

"*What*?" Moss was in no mood.

"I were you, I wouldn't cut no farts."

SEVENTEEN

The cell wasn't what you'd call a promising prospect. In fact, it promised depression and unpleasantness; an ancient stone dungeon made even less cheerful by a crosshatching of graffiti nicely set-off by a collection of iron beds, filthy mattresses, and a slop bucket on which a mangy inmate sat with his greasy, tattered pants around his ankles.

From another bucket, only slightly less foul, an apparently retarded inmate dished vile swill into several dented, grungy bowls. Several prisoners sat around eating the slop with their fingers.

The door was medieval: squat and thick with a barred peephole about a foot square. Two guards in a funkier version of the local cops' suntan uniforms kicked the door open, shoved Jim Dandy and Doc sprawling into the room, then slammed the door shut with a very final kind of clang. Both were battered, bloodied, and unimpressed with the ambiance. They surveyed their comeuppance ruefully, Doc in weary resignation, Jimmy with his usual childlike interest. The other prisoners froze to stare at them. Except for Raul, the inevitable big, animalistic cell leader, who continued to spoon the mess into his matted beard with his filthy mitts.

Jimmy completed his scan of their new home and turned to Doc, "I just have to say it, Ollie..."

"I know, I know: this is the real Cuba most tourists never see."

"And," Jimmy said with emphasis, "We're just in time for chow."

He strolled over to the retarded inmate, who was

staring at him with his mouth drooling open. He picked up two bowls and held them out to be filled, asking in twisted Brit accent, "Please, sir. Could we 'ave some more?"

The inmate gazed at Jim in wonder as he plopped swill into the bowls, and Jimmy carried them back over to where Doc sat against the wall. He handed over one bowl and joined him squatting against the old stone blocks.

Raul backhanded dribble off his beard and dropped his bowl for the retard to scrabble for. He caught the eye of Felix, an inmate shorter, but no less abominable, than himself. He jerked his chin at the newcomers and Felix, an obvious second banana in a tough room, spoke up. "So are you assholes *Yanquis*?"

Doc nodded at the less than brilliant conclusion. "*Pues, si.*"

Jimmy took an opposite posture. "*Yankee*? Fuck no, Hairball. I'm a born rebel, a grayback from way back, a Dixie cup collector, and a drawlin', yawlin', sprawlin' mess a' harmony and grits. I'm a rebel, man."

Raul looked to Felix for help with a matter obviously over his head.

"A rebel?" Raul rumbled. "Is there another rebellion already?" He motioned Felix closer. Other inmates drew into a huddle around him, glancing towards the Americans as they muttered.

"So here we are," Jimmy said cheerfully. "A humble cell with no food worth eating, and nothing to do. You're just wetting your pants over the chance to catch up on fasting and meditating and mortifying the flesh, huh?"

"Well, I'd hoped, but never in my wildest dreams..."

"I'm a bit mortified my own self. How many times is this they've chumped us out?"

"Depends on how big a "they" you mean."

"And how many times you been burned sniffing after Jude?"

"A gentleman doesn't count."

"Don't count for much, I'd say," Jimmy sniffed. He examined his bowl without his usual celebratory reaction towards food. "But you bein' such a gentleman an' all, what kind of wine goes with swill?"

Doc looked into his own bowl. "Maybe a gray Riesling."

"I'll stick to eatin' rats, I guess. They don't move as much." Jim laid his bowl aside in disgust.

"Have you ever eaten a raw rat?"

"Course not," Jimmy scoffed. "I fuck 'em first."

"Softens them up, I suppose?"

"Li'l touch of ol' Tenderizer always makes the flesh more willing."

Raul and Felix approached as they chatted, both scowling. A knot of inmates formed up behind them.

"So you don't like the food?" Felix demanded.

"Well," Doc said judiciously, "It hardly lives up to the ambiance and service."

Raul didn't follow that, but didn't see any need to. "We don't like you. You're *Yanqui* spies and you're going to die."

"Well, sure," Jimmy allowed. "But not today. Let's hunker down and talk it over a little bit."

"No more time to talk." Raul glowered ominously and the inmates moved closer.

Even out in the corridor, separated from the cell by three feet of stone, it was obvious that there was a major commotion going on in the cell where they'd just dumped those stupid *Yanquis*. A guard ran to open the hatch over the peephole, looked inside and became alarmed. He reached for his keys and called for back-up.

When they opened the door, they were greeted by the sight of Jim Dandy, shirt torn and grinning, slamming together the heads of the last two prisoners left standing. Cautiously, the guards moved towards him. He dropped his two cellmates and came quietly.

Doc moved beside him, waiting to be shackled. "Guy's probably doing forty years and doesn't have time to talk."

Jimmy launched into a fine baritone in homage to The Coasters.

"Gonna get caught, just you wait and see.
Why's everybody always picking on me?"

Doc entered a similar cell as unceremoniously as he'd showed up in the first, propelled onto his face by two guards who resented disturbances. He came to his feet and looked around. Same décor, fewer prisoners but of much larger size and ferocity. He stood at the door waiting it out. After a drawn-out pause, the biggest inmate yawned, sat up and appeared to notice Doc for the first time.

"A *Yanqui*?" he asked in false astonishment. "Here?"

Doc, with plenty of ruefulness still on hand, just shrugged. "That's about the size of it, *amigo*."

"What the hell are you doing here?"

Doc looked around the hell-hole and shrugged. "Well, you know... we came for the booze and drugs and pussy."

Looking perplexed, but expectant, the big guy fed him the straight line. "We don't have that stuff here, you dumshit."

Doc ruefully admitted, "I was misinformed."

The cell leader stared at him for a moment, incredulous, then started a long, booming laugh. Slapping the other inmates about their heads and shoulders as they joined him in whooping it up. Finally he drew a breath and came back to Doc.

"You're a funny guy, asshole. Come here, tell us your story. Want some water? Or maybe a little Champagne?" He laughed at his own joke and everybody joined in.

"Just a little water," Doc said.

"*Aguita*?" He keyed in on Doc's Spanish. "You talk like a Mexican. Well, okay, wet your whistle. The pussy will have to wait. I haven't had any Yankee booty for years."

"Oddly enough, me either," Doc told him seriously.

Whooping in laughter, the big guy practically rolled on the filthy floor. "Me, neither. You hear that? I *love* this asshole."

Jim's detention room was a great deal smaller than the original one, and the four inmates inside even bigger and more depraved. The evident leader was reclining on the best of the crappy mattresses, a sleek, menacing, urban type with a major build and pantherish moves. He slid off his pallet; a graceful, fey killer. He approached Jim and eyed him up and down. In a very heavy accent he asked Jimmy, "You are political."

"Naw," Jim demurred. "Just good old criminal scum like your own selves."

The leader scanned his bodily more closely. "You have big muscles, true?"

"Wal, I try to keep buffed up."

"You are a whise guy? A tough guy?"

"Nah, just a guitar bum. How about you? Work out much?"

"I am estuden of martials artes."

"That so? You study Bruce Lee?

"*En absoluto.* Definite."

"Chuck Norris?"

"For hours."

"How 'bout James Brown?"

That put a pause to the leader's belligerent lean-in. He thought it over, suspicious. "I never hear about James Brown."

"You messin' with me, cousin? Never heard of the Sex Machine? The Sultan of Soul? The hardest working man in the bizness any damn day? Comes on like this."

Jim's feet slid over the ringleader's toes. Simultaneously, he bobbed forward and screamed into the inmate's face with a "Brownian" movement. "OooooWOOOOOOO!"

The leader jerked away, but his nailed-down feet cause him to topple over backward. Jimmy nimbly stepped on his Adam's apple and yelled again, also in the style of Brown. "Get *down*!"

Two of the top dog's henchmen, who'd been right behind him, moved to help him, but Jim snatched them by their throats and jacked them on up, still singing,

"Gonna do a thang here called the Tighten Up."

He danced, making musical sound effects and interjecting soul grunts as the two henchmen passed out. He dropped them on top of their former leader and looked a question at the fourth inmate, who shook his head and sat down. Jim sauntered over to the least worst mattress and took a leisurely seat. "Archie Bell and the Drells," he remarked conversationally. "Atlantic Records, 1968."

EIGHTEEN

The printer console shuddered, then slid away from the wall, pulling a section of paneling with it. Herman Moss peered out from behind it, wary behind an UZI. He scanned the room, listened carefully, then reached back into the hidey hole for the other rifles. He cast a last disgusted look at the bodies he'd sat beside in the dark for hours and edged the printer back into position. Sticking the UZI in his waist, he slung two AK's and held the other at port arms as he moved silently towards the stairs.

Moss eased in the window of the Hotel Tania. Once inside he moved to the bed and squatted to reach under it for his waterproof case. Suddenly Sancha sat up in the bed, naked, and embraced him. He recoiled and jerked the UZI up into her face. Both recoiled violently, shaken up. He spat out, "Shit. Piss, Motherfucker. *Suka*! *Sukyin* fuckin' *syn*!"

That snapped Sancha out of her startle. Wide-eyed, she asked, "*Suka*? Me? Sure, I'm a whore, but how come you speak *Ruso*?"

Moss was suddenly attentive, as well. "What'd you say?"

Switching to Russian, she said, "So you speak Russian?"

"And so do you!" He was understandably confused by that, but excitedly switched to Russian himself. "Amazing!"

Sulking torridly, Sancha said, "Incredible. So you can say more than call me a slut."

"Huh?" His Russian was coming back strong, like he'd kept up with it for years. "No, I was just mad. Hey, how come you speak Russian?"

"It's the international language of whores," she purred. When his jaw dropped she chuckled. "No, silly, they made us take it in school. Totally useless to most people. I kept it up, you know... lots of sailors."

"Man, this is great!" Moss exclaimed. Then, in Russky, "Then you can understand me, can help me."

She regarded him critically. "I'm not so sure. Your accent is pretty awful. Even for a *Negro*."

Moss eyed her. "Smart-assed bitch. Figures." He went back to their common tongue, "Listen, honey," he blurted. "I need your help. Doc and Earl need it, actually. We did Calavera, if that's what you want to keep calling him, but then the army got 'em."

"*Ay, cabrón!*" Sancha's alarm was intense and sexy. "Put them in Pedregal, the army prison. I'll find out."

"Any way to get them out of there?"

Sancha gave him a pitying look. "You're even crazier than most *negros*, aren't you?"

Moss pulled the case out as she dressed. Gathering her purse and few odd clothing items, mostly of the very minimal intimate variety, she headed for the door, but stopped with her hand on the knob and turned to look at Moss.

"Maybe we can get them out."

"So now you getting crazy, too? Even for a Latina?"

"Nobody ever tried it before."

"Nobody? Ever?"

She rolled her eyes. "This is Cuba. A blockaded island. Where do you go if you break out?"

Moss stared out the window into the night. "Good motherfuckin' question."

Moss sat at the table with his Walkman on the table in front of him, swigging rum and puffing a cigar while waiting. Sancha had been interested in the walkman/radio at first, especially with the cunning antennae Moss had reeled out of it. But waiting bored her, and she sprawled on the bed, leaning up against the wall.

Suddenly a beep sounded, lights flashed, and the tape went into fast-forward record, emitting a shrill buzz. He rewound it, flipped a switch, pushed PLAY.

Sancha came off the bed and over to the table as the a crackly, high-tech voice came out of the speaker.

"Copy situation," it intoned. "Confirm terminate objective? Return and debrief. Re rescue of operatives: Negative. Repeat, negatory on rescue. Come in now, alone. Out."

She didn't understand, but took her cue from his face;troubled, then glowering like a thunderhead. She sat down on the vanity stool, looking at him.

He scowled, the growled, "Negatory, huh? Nega fuckin tory. Assholes."

He drummed his fingers on the table for a long moment, then snapped. "Well, dig. Fuck negatory. Know what I'm saying?"

He slumped lower in his chair and grabbed a glass, frowning and fulminating. "Fuck that negatory shit."

He turned to Sancha, watching him from the vanity.

"Okay, Honey, where do we start?"

She gave him a sexy, eyelid-dropping smile. "First thing: make up." She turned to the mirror and started applying her eyes.

NINETEEN

The guards supervising the trustees hauling the morning dose of swill to the cells motioned them to stop the barrow of slops in front of the big timbered door, opened the peephole, and peered inside. The cell was apparently empty. But before they could react in alarm, Jim Dandy's head popped up at the peephole, singing.

"Well, there's a man in the funny papers we all know," he trolled, then ducked down out of sight as the heads of the previous cell leader and his henchmen popped up singing, in wretched accents and pitch.

"Alley Oop, Oop. Oop, Oop. Oop."

Jimmy's head immediately replaced theirs. *"He lived back a way long tiiime ago."*

Instantly his backup singers were up and on, *"Alley Oop, Oop. Oop, Oop. Oop."*

The guards were paralyzed, staring as he came back up with, *"He don't eat nothing but a bearcat soup."*

The inmate chorus popped up again, *"Alley Oop, Oop. Oop, Oop. Oop."*

The guards grabbed their keys and started unlocking the door. As they rattled the huge keychain, Jim's clear baritone echoed down the musty corridor, *"And this cat's name is Alley Oop."*

The henchmen were right on time with *"Alley Oop, Oop. Oop, Oop. Oop,"* but the guards had pushed the door open by then, knocking them down.

The grabbed Jim, who didn't resist as they frog-marched him towards the stairs. Except to keep singing. *"Alley Oop, he's the baddest cat ever was alive."*

Back in the cell, a cry rose up. *"Alley Oop!"*

"Wears clothes from a wildcat's hide."

"Alley Oop!"

Jim's voice dwindled somewhat as they tumbled him down the steps, but still echoed up the stone stairwell. *"He's the king of the jungle jive."*

His new recruits wailed after him, *"Alley Oop!"*

The last utterance heard from Jim Dandy on that tier of the dungeon was a wildman scream, *"Look at that caveman go!"*

Few inmates heard, much less appreciated, his afterword, "Tip of the Hatlo hat to the Hollywood Argyles, Lute Records, 1962."

Jim, sporting a few new facial bruises, sat against the wall of an anteroom, under the gun of a guard sitting backwards in one of the rude wooden chairs. He was idly amusing himself with rhythmic clanks of the shackles on his wrists and ankles when Doc entered the room almost horizontally, thrown through the door by two hulking guards. He caught himself and managed to hit the opposite wall with his back without falling, even though he was also cuffed and leg-ironed. The three guards smirked at them and the one in the chair motioned him to sit beside Jimmy. He backed into the wall and slid down it, giving Jim an exasperated glance.

Jim nodded companionably. "Looks like we're grounded, Beav."

"In the office for fighting. Why is my life always stuck in junior high school?"

"Hell, they popped me just for starting a glee club."

Doc shook his head sorrowfully. "Ridiculous. When

glee is outlawed, only outlaws will be gleeful."

"Exactly my point, pardner. Any moron could see this place needs all the cheering up it can get."

Two different burly turnkeys, bigger and better dressed than the dungeon guards, stomped in to scoop up both the Americans and herd them to an inner door, which they opened, pushed them through, then slammed behind them.

Inside the warden's office, Jimmy and Doc were not responding adequately to a fairly long and tedious sweat-out: standard criminal grilling mixed with absurd political accusations and recriminations. A general in the Cuban regular army was glaring at them from the chair behind the old mahogany desk, while the warden sat on his own desk, tapping it suggestively with a braided leather riding crop. Jim handled this attention by stifling yawns and Doc kept buffing his nails on his sleeve and looking at the clock. Aside, Jim muttered, "These chumps wouldn't even make the JV hassling team in Nairobi, huh?"

The General didn't take well to commentary and blustered, "As you say in your rotten country, I smell a rat."

Jim laughed. "As we also say, He who smelt it, dealt it."

The warden stiffened and moved towards him with the crop raised, but there was a knock at the door. Both officers glanced at it, looking questions at each other. The door creaked open and a nun entered shyly, her head lowered and hidden by her surplice.

"Sister," the general said testily, "We are very busy just now. Could we speak some other time?"

The nun floated softly over to the desk, making

benedictory motions.   At the desk she took the Warden's riding crop in hand and ran her fingers along it erotically. She shocked both men (and Jim and Doc, too, for that matter) by saying, "What a wonderful *stick* you have. And this uniform is so stimulating."

Taken highly aback, the warden stammered, "Thank you, Sister... what is your name anyway?" He'd realized by then that it wasn't the usual Sister Julieta who came to see about treating the inmates' ills.

The nun's posture shifted from meek to dominant as she threw back her head and tossed her shoulders, dropping her habit to reveal the prime body of Sancha clad only in fantasy dominatrix drag, her long hair whipping, her net-stockinged legs spraddled, and her hand returning with urgency to the whip. The Cubans were transfixed by her display of black leather, chains, studs and mucho flesh--Doc's eyes were drawn to where she discarded her habit--right on his feet.

"Uh, Sister..." the general stammered.   "Can you please wait outside?"

"Cool!" Jimmy crowed. "Dig Twisted Sister."

"Aw, be a sport," Sancha wheedled, plying the officers with her wide eyes and even wider breasts. "Let me stay. I just adore the sound of a good whipping."

She punctuated her remarks by plastering herself onto the Warden, her hand on the crop and using the double grip to lightly swat herself on the thigh. The Warden was overcome in spite of himself--obviously trying to figure out how to get rid of her without letting her get out of his clutches.

"The man has no respect for the Church Lady," Doc noted disapprovingly.

Turning his confusion on his prisoners, the warden spun and barked, "Shut up, *yanqui* scum!"

Sancha regarded the pair with a sultry simper. "And

these cuties? Who might they be?"

The general spoke loudly and gruffly, trying to get his interrogation back on track. "The are gringos, spies, killers, idiots."

Jimmy sighed, "Fraid we can't much argue with that last one."

Thundering, the warden yelled, "Keep silent!"

"Hey, cool," Jimmy replied, "You got the right to remain silent and everything, huh? Just like real countries?"

Doc decided to just muddy the waters. "And, hey, what are you charging us with? What crime was committed?"

"I won't even get into why we aren't seeing the American consul," Jim sniffed, "Or why no mint on my pillow."

The general was on his feet, flushed, pointing at Jimmy, "Listen, assholes! I ask the questions. And you'd better hope you have the answers!"

"Okay, Alex," Jim allowed easily. "I'll take Krazy Kommy Kooks for two hundred pesos."

Doc reached into the folds of the dumped nun habit and came up with his shorty shotgun. "And what do you know? The daily double."

The general made a swat at his holster, but Doc pointed both barrels right at his eyes, holding the sawed-off at arms length, and he thought it over. The warden tried to lurch into action, but by the time he struggled free from Sancha's cloying embrace, he found himself looking into the bore of his own pistol in her hands. Picking pockets was another job skill she'd acquired in childhood.

Jim exploded off the wall, rocking over his knees to hop flat-footed to his feet. A second hop took him to the desk, where he swung his legs around and grabbed the warden's gun away and flipped it to Sancha. She stuck it artlessly into the top of her garter belt.

Keys were quickly found and the two officials ended up wearing their own shackles, gagged with their own trousers.

"Leather Nun to the rescue," Jim enthused. "Know how many times I've had this fantasy?"

Doc smiled. "*Deja* freakin' *vu*."

Doc and Jim manhandled the two Cubans around the desk and over to the door, shuffling them along with guns held at their backs. Doc cased the door and peeked out, then opened it wider for a longer look. He suddenly leaped through and returned seconds later dragging an unconscious guard by his collar and holding an AK 47, which he handed to Jim.

He turned to Sancha, who was posing in her sex pistols gear, "Nice going, Sancha. Is there a next step to all this?"

"Of course there is," she beamed. "You take me away from all of this."

TWENTY

A runcible taxi--a late fifties Rambler American--was tucked under the shadow of two trees, just outside the cleared lane that surrounded the prison. A crude wood and cane ladder twice its length was lashed to the roof, despite increasingly profane efforts to dislodge it. Yanking at the knots and cursing in English, Russian and Jive, Moss jerked his head up as an alarm sounded inside the walls. He looked up with the expression of a man who expects things to just keep worse.

He was distracted from his dark ruminations by a muffled thumping from the trunk of the old Rambler. Stepping to the rear of the car and leaning over the rear deck, he growled deep in his chest like a pissed-off jungle cat. The thumping stopped at once.

Moving up the other side of the car, Moss stood on the back of an unconscious sentry wearing the hat and uniform of the prison. The extra height evidently helped, because the twine came loose and he was able to slide the ladder off the roof. It tobagganed down to the ground and he grunted as he strained to tip it upright. He did not seem to be enjoying any of these pursuits. The ladder tried to fall into the trees and he caught it with a huge effort, proclaiming, "Fuck this gig with *your* dick."

Doc, Jim Dandy, and Sancha had made it to a tier on the outside wall, but were trapped there, plastered against the wall by a spotlight and guns in the hands of the guards who had flocked to the alarm siren. Jim stood in the shelter of the furious general, his beefy hand clapped over his mouth. They all surveyed the scene: the yard, the walls, the guards. It didn't look very good.

"We need something to divert their attention," Doc said, "Something to really blow their minds."

Jimmy nodded, peering into the armed prison yard. He glanced at the others and rolled his eyes upward, bitching, "So why's everybody looking at me? You think Sancha's not diverting?"

"She needs a followup act."

"Well, okay," Jimmy said sulkily. "But just this once."

He struck a super hero pose, and glided down the parapet, dragging the apoplectic general with him.

Moss gingerly climbed off the top of the ladder onto a narrow battlement on the wall and pulled the coil of hemp rope off his shoulder. Gazing with foreboding at the higher expanse of wall above him, he groaned. "Indiana Moss, puppet on a string."

He took the rope off over his head, flipped it out onto the ledge and slid a crude anchor out of his waistband.

The jailbreak had fomented a riot of confusion and noise inside the prison. Guards dashed around with guns, orders were snapped, fingers pointed. The spotlight jittered around the position of the escapees, but their tier afforded enough cover that they presented no clear targets. Also, they were lying behind the prone form of the warden, who was so incensed by the reversal of imprisonment they'd had to gag him with his nasty socks. Doc scanned the yard, but was at a loss as to what steps to take. Have to pray to Saint Dandy, he thought.

Suddenly a shrill whistle cut through the furor in the yard and the spotlight cast around, then snapped back to pin Jimmy on a high catwalk, doing a slow dance step with the general, whose windpipe he clasped tightly in a way that looked like some tango variation. He did a daring dip, then spun the general around and peeped out over his shoulder, vamping at the armed mob below. Worse, he started singing, after the influence of Spider Turner.

"*Spotlight on Jim Dandy now, yeah, yeah.*" He kneed the general into a bob, then popped him erect, continuing his vocal performance. "*Singing sweet as ol' candy now, yeah, yeah.*"

A sniper in the courtyard threw up his assault rifle to take a bead, but a commander of some sort knocked it away, feverishly mentioning the general: hero of Africa, bosom friend of *El Jefe*, himself.

Jimmy switched to his Elvis impression, one of his strongest, since White Trash was his native tongue. "Thank you, thank you very much. I appreciate you having me into your stinking fucking shithole tonight. And let's have a warm Havana hand for my puppet buddy Fidelito, here. Can you see my lips move when I talk?"

He released the general's throat and he screamed, "*No disparen! No disparen!*"

"Wasn't that great folks?" Jimmy continued his Late, Smarmy Elvis shtick. "It's Spanish for "Don't shoot my ass off", but you knew that. Didn't see his lips move, did you? It's that damn beard. I hear Fidel has collagen and you can't tell."

Doing a disco hip bump, he got the general's booty shaking as he launched into a balls-out version of The Animals' "We Gotta Get Out Of This Place". Doc and Sancha, taking him up on the mind-blowing diversion they'd prayed for, were hustling along the tier to a gap

107

that had probably at one time featured a huge coastal cannon. Sancha flopped belly-down into the gap and looked down, almost bumping heads with Moss, who heaved himself up his climbing rope and motioned urgently to them both. Doc choked the warden unconscious and started descending the rope.

As soon as his feet hit the outside ledge, he turned to spot Sancha, who seemed to need no help skinning down the line. Moss rappelled down, leaving the rope in place for Jimmy. He stepped to the battlement, looked below, and froze, mentioning several classes of motherfucker. The ladder he was looking for lay flat on the ground below and a uniformed guard was examining the taxi.

Inside, Jimmy continued his routine, jigging the helpless general around, but had switched to "Jailhouse Rock", which he handled in Las Vegas Imitator form, benefiting from much practice of the Presley repertoire.

In mid chorus, Jim ducked behind a stanchion, giving the general a kick that launched him off the edge into the courtyard. The spotlight, fooled by the motion, followed the general's plunge, settling on his inert form on the cobbles of the courtyard. The spotlight darted down, following the General's fall, and showed him sprawled on the ground.

"Spotlight on yawl's balls now, yeah, yeah." Jim crowed, but when the searchlight snapped back up, he was gone.

On the external parapet, Jim slid down the rope like a counterweight, bouncing over to see what had the others so bummed out. He took in the ladder, the guard, and shook his head judiciously.

"Okay, okay. I know who does all the work around here." He did an easy, flatfooted hop to the top of the chest-high stone railing and assumed the tucked position of a swimmer awaiting the sound of a starting gun.

Moss couldn't believe it. "Jesus, Earl. That jump's impossible."

Jim laughed. "Not for Guitarzan, baby." His muscles bunched super-heroically and he launched a dive out into space, his hands held in front of him like George Reeves. Doc and Moss watched him, imagining the "Flying Music" from the old Superman TV series. He caught a branch, which gave under his weight, then another, which bent in and slammed him against the main trunk.

"Watch out for that tree, Jungle George," Doc said as Jimmy rebounded off the trunk onto a lower limb, then tripped down limbs like Fred Astaire on a staircase, his last hop landing him on the shoulders of the guard, who slammed his jaw on the fender of the cab as he collapsed.

Jim ran to the foot of the wall and pointed up at Sancha. Then suddenly extended his hands straight up and held them there.

Doc snatched Sancha up and held her over the edge, where she exhibited insecurity about being dropped into the night.

"Wait, shit." Moss whispered. "His hands are up. Somebody must have him covered."

Doc chuckled, "Just calling for a fair catch." He dropped Sancha, who fell silently, her novitiate's whore-rags streaming around her.

Jim stepped casually up and grabbed her out of the air. Then hugged her knees as he dropped her torso, swung her behind his back and around to the cradle of his arms. He completed his fifties swing routine by bucking her up in the air, rotating longitudinally, then catching her again.

Speaking to her passionately, he murmured, "Scarlet, I'm ready to carry you over the threshold. Preferably the pain/pleasure threshold."

Sancha giggled and hopped out of his embrace to help him lift the ladder. Doc, then Moss, slid down the ladder on their palms and insteps like firemen.

"Pretty fair catch, actually," Moss said as he knocked the ladder over again and headed for the Rambler. "She's lucky you didn't spike her."

"Saving that, brother. For when we get..." he launched into a deepdish Charlie Rich imitation, "...*behind closed doors.*"

As the escapees ran up to the cab, the thumping from the trunk started again. As Moss ran by the rear end, he slammed his palm down on the trunk lid and it stopped. From below it a pitiful voice moaned, "Ay, Caramba!"

"Shotgun!" Jimmy yelled, but Doc produced the immaculate sawed-off Sancha had smuggled him.

"Already called it."

Jimmy hustled Sancha into the back seat and slid in himself. "Ladies and gentlemen, the King has left the building."

TWENTY-ONE

Moss floored the old car down unfamiliar, pitted roads, pushing the limits just to get away from the lights and shrieking alarms of the prison. He threw a sudden left, piling the other three against the right hand doors, and started a wild descent towards the harbor below. Jimmy applauded and he growled, "Hope the damn 'King' manages to keep his ass outta the building this time, too."

Leaning back, arm around Sancha and copping a feel, Jim Dandy proclaimed, "Just shows one great eternal truth to anybody wants to pick up on it."

"Lay it on me," Doc said as he scanned the road for problems.

"Nothing," Jimmy intoned, "But nothing. Can stop the Duke of Earl."

"You hadda fuckin' ask," Moss grumbled. "Listen, what went down in there?"

"What you think?" Jimmy asked, incredulous, "They jacked us up, beat us down, and fucked us up the butt."

"Aw, no, man..."

"El Reamo Creamo Supremo," Jimmy cited sadly.

"Le Enema Verité," Doc added.

"Ah, shit."

"Well, you know," Doc said, "In a place like that you have to expect a certain amount of hazing."

"What matters," Jimmy said "Is we're the fuck outta there. I'm once again..." his voiced veered up towards Skynardian flight, "...a free bird."

"Don't be singing about it yet, dipstick," Moss countered. "There's still the little matter of getting out of the country. And we got no plan."

"We never did, did we?" Doc asked pointedly. "Not that we knew about."

"Go ahead, rub it the fuck in."

"Herman," Doc said in a quiet, even tone, "Why'd you come in here if you don't even speak Spanish?"

"It was my idea to use you two tools, so I got stuck running you."

"Since Jude wasn't really involved, we got the nod because we had a chance of getting in and because it didn't matter if we got killed."

Moss shrugged at the obvious, "Either way, a few less assholes on the loose. Hate to break it to you."

"Hey," Jimmy said from the back, "We're used to being cannon fodder. But how about you?"

Moss snorted. "Get real."

"You want it like that, fine," Jimmy continued. "But what's your so real thoughts on how they knew we were there? I don't think a regiment stopped by just for a knob job from Absolom."

Doc agreed. "I get a heavy impression everybody there was supposed to end up dead."

"So why didn't we?"

"They couldn't find Absolom's body. Figured we could tell them. And who and why. You should've seen who was talking to us about it."

"They probably don't get much chance to practice English interrogations."

Doc changed the subject, "Anyway, do 'they' have any plan for getting out of this?"

"Well, kind of. They told me to bail on you fuckers. But I lost my damn mind and came after you."

"Insane," Doc agreed.

"Aw Herman," Jimmy simpered. "You do care."

"Fuck you, Earl. I just hate to..."

"Whoa up!" Jimmy cut in imperatively. "Draw your brakes, Herm. I gotta hot flash."

The car skidded to a stop across from a pier where a naval launch lay moored to a small concrete pier. A smallish vessel, it looked well-maintained. It was totally dark on board.

Pointing through the back window, Jimmy asked, "What the hell is that?"

Sancha peered out, her chin resting on his shoulder. "It's a navy launch they use to take Fidel on inspection tours."

"Well then," Jimmy chortled. He reached up to pull an imaginary bell rope as he sang ala Kingsmen, *"Baby let me take you onna...Sea Cruise."*

The launch's dock was deserted except for a single sentry doing a desultory patrol. He snapped to full attention, however, when Sancha stepped smartly onto it, swiveling towards him like a sailor's wet dream on land legs. He was all eyes and ears for her when Jimmy exploded out of the water behind him like a Sea World orca, vaulting up on the dock, knocking him down, but arresting his fall with a cord around his neck.

The guard fell to his knees, dropping his carbine as Jimmy tightened the improvised garrotte. Sancha stooped to grab the gun, stepped back to watch the man struggle helplessly.

Jim sang softly ala Elvis,

"Well, I slip this lil sucker around his throat.

And when I bend a string that's all she wrote."

He relaxed the cord, pushing the sailor to his face and shoving him under an upturned dinghy with his feet.

"And he's gone, gone, gone.
Flopping like a catfish on a dock.
Gone gone gone,'
Cause of messing 'round with Jimmy and Doc."

Sancha peered at the fallen sailor, half-covering him with his own rifle. "Is he dead?"

"Nah, I just like to leave 'em..." Jimmy inhaled melodramatically in the manner of Jerry Lee Lewis..."Breathless."

Doc, dripping wet, was pushing a second sentry out a hatch in the launch's aft cabin. Jim and Sancha entered in time to hear the splash outside. Moss stuck his head through a starboard porthole to announce. "All clear out here. Just the two. Can we get this thing started?"

"Just cast off them lines, swabby," Jim Dandy commanded. "Lemme do a little hot-wiring here."

He ducked out of the wheelhouse, dropping below as Doc ran a check of controls and flipped switches. Sancha ran her own checklist, poking around in cabinets. She reached into one, smiling, and turned cradling a bottle of rum. Muffled by the bulkheads, the engine coughed, then started.

Doc grinned. "Hot-wired and conspiring to joyride."

Jimmy's voice echoed out of the brass speaking tube on the bulkhead. "Damn good thing I majored in Piratical Sciences at LSU."

Doc spoke directly into the tube. "Give us quarter speed ahead, give me a chance to check the handling and get us pointed out to sea."

"Aye, aye, mi capitan."

The launch jerked, then came smoothly underway. "Jimmy sang through the speaking tube.

"Ride Captain, ride.

114

Upon your mystery ship.

"Hell, if you're going to sing," Doc told him, "You might as well give it full ahead. We'll just cowboy it out of here."

"Louie, Louie, matey," Jimmy snapped with nautical briskness. "Jive ho. Shiver me testes and jizm the mains'l." He launched into a parody of "The Walloping Window Blind",

"Oh we sailed on a reach to a sandy beach

For to dig the bearded clam..."

Doc grimaced and stuffed a rag in the tube, stifling Jim's hornpipe. The launch accelerated, moving towards its hull speed with Doc intent at the wheel. Sancha looked around, peered out the ports, shrugged, and knocked back a belt of the rum.

As the launch spanked nicely past the castle at the mouth of Havana's magnificent harbor and pointed out to open sea, the Eastern sky was just lightening into dawn.

TWENTY-TWO

The little launch cut effortlessly through the low, slow swell of the open Caribbean, rolling over the sun-sparkle in the general direction of Key West, but with the Cuban mainland still visible behind it. Jim and Doc stood on top of the wheelhouse with binoculars, Doc scanning the horizon abaft, Jim focusing on the foredeck below, where Sancha lolled nearly naked, catching a few rays.

Doc pulled his attention away from her lush flesh. "Damn. Here they come."

"Took 'em long enough to figure it out and get after us."

"Well, it won't take them long to catch us. They're big, heavily armed, and twice our speed. Have to be making thirty knots."

Jim serenely scanned the big gray naval vessel in pursuit of them. "Rockin' good news. We snatch their boat and get home in half the time."

Doc leaned over to speak in the wheelhouse window. "Hey Herman, lash the wheel on this course and come up. We have to decide what to do. Bring the guns."

"Sounds like you already decided," Jim wryly observed.

"What, you want to take a vote?"

Jim called out loudly to Sancha, "Yo, Chiquita! You vote for dying, or going back to Cuba in chains?"

Sancha came off the deck smoothly and stared back at the pursuing ship. She walked back towards the wheelhouse, watching it draw closer, bristling with armed marines.

116

"Shit," she spat, "It's the Camaquey. The piggiest crew afloat, all just dying to fuck us up."

"This gal knows her sailors," Jim beamed proudly. "So how you vote, toots?"

Sancha brandished the sentry's carbine overhead, shaking it. "The full metal ticket."

Moss emerged from the hatch, lugging an armful of guns. "You *votin'* this shit? We ain't got a chance."

"Or even a quorum," Doc noted for the record.

"Lemme tell you I size it up, " Jimmy told them. He selected a Brazilian H&K from Moss, checked the magazine, and slammed it back home. "I say, Lock and load..." He howled like Rick Derringer,

"Lock and load, hootchie koo
Lawd yo' mama bites my fuse."

His vocal endeavors were cut off by a hail of small arms fire from the deck of the Camaguey. He dove behind the wheelhouse, along with the rest, as the Cuban marines raked them with automatic fire. The deck gun lobbed a shell near enough to splatter the decks and ring the hull like a bell, then two more, equally close.

Jimmy popped up, the rifle at his shoulder, happily singing as he worked at peppering the cruiser's deck. His baritone didn't quite resemble the Rivingtons, but he had the melody down pat,

"Pa pa pa, oom, mow mow,

Pa pa pa, oom, mow mow.

Pa pa pa, oom, mow mow,

Pa pa pa, oom, mow mow."

Doc had joined him in pouring lead at the larger vessel, but was already thinking about the fact that they had very little spare ammo. He squatted in the shelter of the wheelhouse to reload as Jimmy also popped down, pulling out another magazine. He howled, just like the record. "Pa pa, pa pa, OOOOOOOO!" Then popped back up to continue mow-mowing the Cuban vessel.

The fight continued fierce, with occasional outbreaks of musical comedy. The boys were taking a toll, even Sancha scoring a few hits, but the firepower advantage was far too great and the situation had Last Stand written all over it.

There were fires breaking out on the deck by then, and smoke ghosting out of the portholes below. The fusillade had eliminated most of the cover on board, pushing everybody into a forlorn huddle behind the wheelhouse, which was also being slowly chewed away by the withering marine fire. Battle-worn but determined, the four fought on.

Suddenly Sancha jumped up and shook her fist, defiantly howling, "*Cuba libre*!"

Not to be outdone, Jimmy reared back and hollered like a hog caller, "Rock and Roll will never die!"

Even the dour Moss was swept up by the mood, yelling, "We shall overcome!"

Doc checked his shotgun and stuck it in his belt, then picked up the last loaded assault rifle. He noticed the other three looking at him expectantly and sighed. Wearily, he raised his fist. "Bird lives!"

Jimmy and Moss regarded him sourly, Jimmy snorting, "Damn jazz hags. Some words to live by, Doc."

"Oh, you think we're going to live?"

Jimmy dropped down on his heels and looked him straight in the face. "I have such hopes, Hoss." He swept a dramatic arm to the North and triumphantly announced, "Since, we got the U.S. Calvary to the rescue."

Doc swung his head around to see the welcome sight of a U.S. Coast Guard cutter bearing towards them. The Camaquey was already bearing off and accelerating. Doc glanced at Jim, who winked, then did a Coasters number.

"Aaa, aaa...

And then along came Jones.

Sweet shuckin', slow fuckin' Jones."

Doc sagged back against the bulkhead, his rifle falling into his lap as he grinned. "Never thought I'd be glad to see the Coast Guard catch me."

Sancha was taking her own interest in the approaching cutter. "Those *yanqui* sailors sure dress nice."

"Better than a floating Shriner's convention, huh, Babycakes?" Jimmy asked her rhetorically, then spoke aside to Doc. "Wish she'd get her mind off work and just enjoy the cruise."

The crew of the cutter, however, appeared anything but friendly. They'd approached cautiously, covering the smaller vessel with everything from heavy machine guns to M-16's. Their cool gray hull loomed over the sinking launch, rocket launchers aimed, armed sailors at the ready.

On the bridge, three stories above the fugitives on the launch, a much-decorated captain and several other officers, all wearing holstered pistols, leaned over to examine this oddball catch. A junior officer stepped out with a bullhorn and tapped it, blasting an electronic bark. Highly amplified and military, he commanded, "Put down your weapons. Keep your hands in sight. Prepare to be boarded. We will fire at any sign of resistance."

The four had already laid down their arms and kept their hands readily visible. Jim Dandy spoke up, his voice carrying easily up to the officious officer. "Hey, Slick. Can't you see by our outfits we aren't Cuban navy?"

"Or at least by our haircuts and personal grooming," Doc added.

The junior officer glanced at the captain and replied at full bull volume, "Negative. You are suspected drug traffickers. Stand by to be boarded and show manifest."

"Now you're talking, Nephew," Jimmy bellowed. "Any dope you find we'll go halves."

"As you were!" The J.G. was not liking this backchat in front of his captain. "Identify yourselves."

Doc spoke up, deciding he'd better do the talking. "My name's Hardesty, this is Jimmy Dan Earl. We escaped from a Cuban prison and are trying to get home. That's Herman Moss. He's a CIA agent, but that's supposed to be sort of a secret."

The J.G. Pondered a second and came up short on amplified responses. He turned to his superiors and said, "Orders, Sir?"

The grizzled captain leaned over the rail and squinted at the boatload of survivors. He started to speak, then held out his hand, which was quickly filled with the younger officer's bullhorn. In a rich southern accent he barked, "Did you say Jimmy Dan Earl?"

"No," Jimmy told him, "He did. You can just call me Jim Dandy."

"Did you ever play football for Louisiana State University?"

"I had that privilege for four fine years. You aren't here to collect for that fucking alumni fund, are you?"

"I might forget a name or face," the captain boomed, "But not three touchdowns in the Peach Bowl. Especially against that coonass Arkansas."

"If I coulda done her on them Nebraska Cornholers, we'da got Cotton Bowl."

"You did your share, son. Come aboard and tell your sorry story."

Moss gave Jimmy a sidelong look. "You were a Tiger?"

"Still am, old son. Tiger a go-go, and tigerish on America. Been known to breed in captivity. 'Scuse me now, I gotta go dish grits with some scum alum."

Two sailors threw a hawser down from the main deck and Jimmy made it fast to a deck cleat on the foundering launch, then grabbed it and went up hand over hand.

"He's very big with the old boy network," Doc told Moss, deadpan.

"Shit, I guess. They'll probably give him the damn ship and he'll scam us into painting it for him."

Doc eyed the looming cutter. "Might look pretty cool in metalflake with a racing stripe."

TWENTY-THREE

A black chauffeured limousine that might as well have had "government carpool" scrawled all over it pulled out of the barrio night and slid up to the curb in front of possibly the shabbiest two-story stucco in a Latino neighborhood that consisted of little else but. It might be thought of as a "safe house", but looked like a crack fortress, except for the proud banner across the roofed front porch: *Grupo 18 de Junio.*

The rear curb door opened and Simms stepped out, dressed as if for an embassy ball, and quartered the street for bad omens. He became highly intent when a the door of a nondescript rental sedan opened across the street, trying to see in the windows while keeping his own door open in case. Herman Moss stepped out of the other car and moved towards Simms, purposeful and radiating anything but buddy bonding.

Simms was deeply shocked to see him, but showed nothing of that as he smiled warmly. "Herman! Boy, is this a surprise."

"I'll bet it is."

Simms headed around the car to meet Moss. "We didn't expect you back so soon. But here you are! Took out Muto! You pulled it off, my man."

Moss stopped, squared off at his partner. "Amazing, under the circumstances."

"I'm sure you have a lot of questions about the whole operation. The debriefing..."

"Just one, actually. Where's the woman? Mayfield. You have her?"

Simms laughed dismissively. "I think there are bigger issues that that on the table. Listen, we have to..."

"She's here, isn't she? Right up in that crib. How many people know about this jivetime fuckup? You thought you'd get away with this?"

The bonhomie fell away, but Simms continued smiling, "Why not? Perez is solid, those two cowboys are vanished, and here we sit. We *did it,* Herman. Eliminated Absolom Muto with no loss, no comeback, no compromise. Fucking genius. We're going to ride this one all the way up, Herm. We're made."

"Yeah, sure. But now it's over and it's time to break it down and get over it, dig? We'll forget some of the "irregularities" here, kind of skim over who got ass-out down there. Just give her up and all is copacetic. You hear what I'm saying, here?"

Simms shook his head patronizingly. "You're not aware of the bigger picture yet, Herman. We've got other uses for her. For one thing, how am I going to release an British journalist kidnapped by the CIA? Besides, she's the next best thing to Hanoi Jane. You realize how many times she's fucked us up, starting with Nam and most lately the Contra operation? I've got a three point plan for her and using her for shithead bait was only Part One."

"Why didn't I guess that? Well, fuck you partner, I'm going in there and getting her out right now."

He headed for the door, Simms standing aside and motioning him by like a maitre'd. But as soon as he'd taken two steps past him, Simms jumped up and gave him a flying karate kick between the shoulder blades, knocking him flat. Moss rolled and came to his feet cocked and bobbing like a welterweight.

Simms fell into a martial arts stance, moving very classy and dealing some deadly blows. But Moss just waded in, blocked everything he threw, grabbed him, and chucked him out of the way. Then turned and

123

walked toward the door.   Simms, choking with humiliation, pulled a gun from under his tux jacket, started to say something, then just plugged Moss from behind. Moss went down like a dumpload of bricks.

Simms got to his feet, dusted off his tux, and stood over him, gloating. "You thought you could beat me, Moss? At anything? You must be losing it. Ultimately you're just muscle around here. Just a field nigger."

"And where'd we shiftless honkies be without 'em, I ask you?"

Simms whirled smoothly, the pistol thrust out in front of him, busting a pure James Bond.   But Jim Dandy was standing at the corner of the house with an assault rifle pointed at the center of his body mass. He saw movement to his left and glanced away to see Doc sliding along the facade of the house, back to the wall, a sub-machine gun pointed right at him.

He lowered the gun slowly, but jerked it back up as a Cuban thug in camo pants and Gators sweatshirt burst out the front door, responding to the shot that had taken Moss down.   He was crouching over an M-16, eyes wide. Doc clotheslined him right off his feet as he ran past, grabbing the rifle out of his hands as his feet shot up and his ass plunged down.

Jimmy didn't even glance at the disturbance, but Simms evidently thought he should have and made his move. His final move, it turned out: Jim chopped him into a jagged death dance, then spun his Ingram and blew smoke from the barrel.

Jim glanced to see if Doc was covering him, then loped out to grab Herman and haul him to the limo in a high-speed, zig-zagging drag. He dropped him through the back door then gave the chauffeur a look over the back seat. The drivers showed him open hands and wide eyes. "Hey, I just drive for the motor pool, man. Anywhere you want to go."

124

Moss' eyes were fluttering and he wasn't completely staunching the flow of blood from the gaping exit wound, but he gasped, "Air Force hospital at Homestead."

Jimmy was tearing his own shirt up and using it to plug the wound more securely. He yanked off a handful of Moss' shirt and reached under him to plug the sucking entry wound in his lower back. "Ain't that just like a nigger? Gets his dumb ass shot for nothing, then wants to go to a government doctor in a Cadillac."

Weakly, Moss said, "Ain't it just like some honky ofay bitch to get a nigger killed to save his white ass, then make him sit in the back of the bus?"

Knotting the sleeve he'd jerked off the driver's shirt to tie the wads into the wounds, Jim tsked, "Shit, I should left you out the yard to get humped by those Julios and the paper boy."

"Ain't enough you offed my partner, huh?"

Jimmy gently slid him along the seat, smearing the fine leather with blood. "Nuther asshole in desperate need of a death check."

"Yeah, well, show some respect."

"Sure. I'll name one of my kids for you, how's that?"

"I think one black bastard named Herman's plenty enough."

"Probly so." Jim backed out of the car and closed the door, but spoke to the driver through the open window. "Better get him to an ER before he really starts whining."

Jimmy tapped the TV screen on the back of the front seat. "And turn on some Bill Cosby, one those colored shows he can relate to."

Moss was fighting for consciousness, but rallied. "Shit, I done related to your mama."

"She mentioned it was pretty disappointing." Jim

125

banged on the roof of the Cad, which peeled out sharply, then turned and headed for the house. At the corner of the porch he glanced up, then leapt forward, one foot topping the porch rail then launching him out to grab the overhanging gutter. He slid up and over the eave.

Doc maintained his position beside the door, knocked loudly. "Candygram."

A spate of automatic fire took out half the door. "Okay," Doc said softly. "Land shark."

He dropped flat on the porch and reached forward to hold the M-16 at right angles to his body and pointing through the blown-out door. He thumbed the trigger, hosing down the front hallway. More shots and several screams sounding inside.

Doc pushed up on his arms and went to the full military "command voice" beloved by sergeants everywhere. "All I want is the woman. Give her up and we're all home free. Simms is dead. He can't help you now."

More fire greeted his comment. Doc grimaced and got to his feet.

A Cuban-American hood who thought of himself as an international mercenary knelt on the floor, peering out the upstairs window trying to see what was going on under the porch. He could see Simms' body, Hector's red Nikes lying motionless. He craned to see further out, carefully leading with his Brazilian assault rifle. Suddenly the gun disappeared from his hands, bruising his wrists as it flew away, then suddenly thrust back through the window butt-first, knocking him on his ass. Jim Dandy slid through the window like a leopard, a machine gun pointed in each fist. He stood over the Cuban, the muzzle of the rifle indenting his

126

bloody face and smashed nose. Deciding he had the man's full attention, he said, "Give her up, bitch."

Defeated but defiant, the *Marielito* barked, "What the fuck for?"

Jim thought if over cagily. "Most we could go is two third round draft picks to be named later."

That grabbed the fallen warrior, even with his face throbbing in pain and menaced by .223 projectiles. "Who the hell are you, anyway?"

"I'm the hostage fairy, fuckwad!" Jimmy snapped in exasperation. Hand her over and get a dime under your pillow. Do anything else and you get your shit in a sack."

A philosophical break-through occurred to the young Cuban. "Hey, like I give a shit. She's in the bedroom across the hall."

"Proper response, troop." Jimmy popped both guns to one-handed Present Arms and did a snappy about face towards the door. Then spun back around, cautionarily, and said, "Oughta do something about that nose."

He flowed out the door with both guns just begging for trouble. The man on the floor heard more shots in the house and grunts from outside the door, but decided that giving a shit was still totally uncalled for.

The other upstairs bedroom was less shabbily furnished than the one over the front porch, mostly because it had been stripped of furniture in honor of its inmate. A tall, dark-haired woman who could have been a harried thirty or well-preserved forty-five stood against an interior wall, staring at the door, less scared than avidly curious. A professional deformity of journalists like Jude Mayfield.

Suddenly the door swung open, but stayed at right angles to the wall, obscuring her view of who had entered. Her curiosity know no bounds. Whatever she was expecting, it certainly wasn't Jimmy Dan Earl peeping around the edge of the door and bouncing his eyebrows at her like Groucho Marx.

"Oh my God, Jim Dandy," she gasped. "So they've decided to torture me?"

Jim stepped into the room, crossed to the window for a quick scan, then stood where he could see her and cover the doorway. "Naw, there's no justice. They decided to unleash your ass on the world again."

Jude didn't celebrate her freedom much. That curiosity thing. "Now why would they decide that?"

"Cause we told 'em if they didn't we'd get rowdy, I 'spect."

"We? So there's some human intelligence behind all this?"

Jim shrugged deprecatingly. "Well, just ol' Doc."

"Doc? Hardesty? Here?" That seemed to unsettle her more than imprisonment and listening to a mass killing outside her door. "Crikee."

"He'll be up directly," Jim told her. "Case you want to fix your makeup or anything. And hey, try to act a little glad you got rescued, huh? Doc's more into that shining knight shit than I am."

"They were holding me hostage, weren't they? To get Doc to do something awful?"

"Always the quick little study. And Doc was always whipped enuff to go along with it."

"Who'd they want dead this time?"

"Some spade fag."

"What, isn't AIDS fast enough for them?"

"Sometimes they like the personal touch." Doc came

128

into the room casually, his weapons dangling loose in his hands. Everybody around must already be dead, Jude thought.

She looked at him with no sign of the roiling complex of emotions that his very name had conjured up. "Whatever it was, Doc, you shouldn't have."

Jimmy snorted. "*Now* she tells us."

"Well, anyway," Doc said to her as if they were the only people there. Or anywhere. "Here we are again."

"Well, yes, it is here that we are, I suppose."

"I was keying in more on the 'we'. And the 'again'."

"Doc, I'm afraid there was then and here is now."

"Yesterme, yesteryou, huh?"

"You know who you've been around too long when you start talking in song lyrics."

"Hey, Ms. Grunt Goddess," Jimmy drawled in disgust, "We just risked our butts to rescue you. Doesn't that even count for a dry hump in the elevator anymore?"

"I really do appreciate you blokes taking the trouble. But, you know, I was just a pawn to suck you in. If you'd gotten your arses blown off they'd have let me go."

"Damn!" Jimmy slapped his forehead. "Why didn't we think of that? Could've saved everybody a few hassles."

"Really," Doc said. "And they'd have probably posed for pictures for your story about the government kidnapping foreign journalists."

"Probably would have just handed out some stock eight by tens. I really am sorry, Doc. If I can ever help either of you, get hold of me."

"Like a massive hard-on's not an emergency that could use a helping hand."

"Please teach Bonzo the difference between emergencies and disasters."

Doc pondered that one. "Doesn't it have something to do with whether they're natural or not?"

"I think we can rule out anything natural in his case."

"Its my own case I'm pleading here."

"Case closed." She took a deep breath and stepped right in front of him, meeting his eyes with her big, brown serious ones. "Look, don't take it personally, Hardesty. But what you were to me was a soldier. And I spent a lifetime screwing soldiers. Least I could do making a living off you getting killed. I couldn't refuse any of you comfort when you were stuck there in the shit. You're the only one that tried to take it personal."

"You beat the hell out of Bob Hope, I'll say that."

"Step back there, Doc," Jimmy commanded like a traffic cop. "Let me handle this for you. You're too close to the problem here, can't see the forest for the bush."

He turned to Jude, who looked on the border between intrigued and disgusted, and spake thusly: "Look, this man knows you ain't no hound dog; can't you see him peeping at you like a one-eyed cat in a seafood store? He just wants to be your lover, baby, don't wanna be your boss. Just wants you to give a piece a chance is all, just wants to wrap you in his warm and tender legs, wants to help you make it through the night, you know? He just wants to be your everything, wants to be your macho man, be your teddy bear, your handy man, your salty dog, your overnight sensation, your meat puppet, your smooth up criminal...your lip-smacking, ham-slammin, joint-jumpin, nipple-nibblin', boogy-woogy foo'. Just wants to fill your nooks with silly love prongs, be your too live crude, so don't be rude to a heart that's nude. You see what I'm drivin' at?
130

If you had half a heart on your hands and half a hint in your head you'd see a stone white soul over there, just hangin' out drippin' for you. The man loves your agin' ass, worships the spot you sleep on, and you're making him the king of pain. Get a clue, cupcake, and give it the hell up while there's still open offers."

Turning back to Doc, he dropped a humongous wink and burbled, "There you go, kinfolk, did I put you right or what?"

"I knew you'd say that," Jude said. "Look, Doc, it's nothing personal. Just whatever you've got on for me, I'm not worth it."

Jimmy threw his eyes toward the stained ceiling and queried, "What was I just *sayin'*?" He whipped back to Doc and told him, "Take some notes here. The reason you got no luck with women is because you don't know the way to handle them."

Jude's ears pricked up at that. "And just which way is that?" she demanded.

"Every which but loose."

"Why was I even hoping for a little sanity out of you? Either of you?"

"I was hoping you'd be more specific," Doc said candidly.

Jimmy whispered a stage aside, "What it is, brother, you got to catch 'em off guard."

"And if you can't?"

"Then you just have to go off-tackle."

"Will you lads pardon me," Jude asked. "While I go powder my gag reflex? It's been lovely seeing you, Doc."

She strode towards the door as Doc fought his impulse, then gave into it, taking two fast steps to clutch her elbow and turn her to face him. "I had to do some things that really suck to get you out of here," he said, embarrassed to have to plead and bargain, "Things I keep trying to quit doing. It cost me. Can I get five minutes?"

She was embarrassed, too. Not much to ask a former lover after rescuing her from, she had to admit, pretty certain death. She turned to him, hands cradling her elbows in a pose of protective body language.

Doc turned to Jimmy, who was flipping the assault rifle and catching it. "Could you give us a moment alone, here?"

"Alone and defenseless with Ms. Maneater of 1971?" Jim sniffed.

"There's really nothing more to say, Doc," Jude said from behind him.

"Yeah there is," he replied. "Please, Jimmy."

Jim sneered at Jude, did a crisp about face and marched through the door, spinning the rifle in front of him like a baton. In the hall he did a snappy left face and was gone. Doc turned to Jude, who looked uncharacteristically flustered and tight. "What did I tell you in Cam Rahn Bay?" she snapped.

"That you gave it up for fighting boys and as soon as I got on the plane I wasn't one any more."

"And you couldn't just buy that?"

"Why? You're not in the wars any more, either. And why the stupid 'I only do grunts' bit anyway? To make up for making a living out off them dying? Fine. But that's a long time gone. I'm talking about now and tomorrow."

"Yeah, and you're talking shit, GI. There's no happy ever after coming around here. Can't you get that?"

"Only if you say so. I'm here for you right now. I always would be."

Jude shook her head violently, held her hands out as if to ward him off or strike at his face. "You pitiful

132

chump," she rasped. "Here for what? Don't even answer that. I'll do you a favor. I'll tell you the story. Maybe it'll get us off each other's backs."

Doc looked at her warily, shrugged. "It's worth a shot."

"Okay, you know I got captured. And got back." Doc nodded but she was plunging on, talking like a rabbit flees. "The VC took out the platoon I was covering, and I guess they wanted to send somebody a message. I never found out who, or what the message meant. But you know what ended up bugging me the longest?"

Doc stared at her as she talked, not wanting to hear. Now he was the rabbit, mesmerized by the bobbing eyes.

"They didn't even bother to rape me." She tried to mimic an offended pose at that, but it collapsed and she plunged on, inching over to Doc as she spoke faster and faster. "I didn't even mean enough to them for them to take their shitty pyjama pants off. They just stripped me and tied my arms behind me and sat me down on top of a stake they'd pounded into the ground and sharpened with those machete things they carried. I guess I was too light, so they wired some scrap metal to my feet. Then they just walked off."

Doc could no longer watch her face, just bowed his head into the bitter gust blowing out of her.

"They didn't even bother to watch." She gave a tight, jittery smile. "Funny thing, it didn't hurt as bad at first. But every time I took a breath or had a muscle spasm or shiver it settled me down more on the stake. It just kept working up through my pelvis into my guts, a little at a time."

Doc slowly slumped against the wall, staring at his feet. She continued talking as if in a trance, her face smeared with irony over a hard base of despair.

"I guess I was up there a pretty long time, working that thing up into my body, but I missed a lot of the fun by passing out all the time. In between screaming. One nice thing, I didn't lose all that much blood. Apparently one of the positive features about having something tapered shoved into you is that it keeps you from bleeding so much. One of those mixed blessing things."

She seemed to suddenly snap out of something, glanced at Doc leaning on the wall, his hands held over his stomach. She squared off to him and spoke in a very soft, cool tone. "Well anyway, it hadn't killed me by the time some LURP recon guys found me. They sawed the stake off and called in a slick to dust me off. I remember thinking I was like a human corn dog."

She shuddered violently, but got it under control, all the irony falling away. "But that pretty well put paid to my sex life. A couple of surgeries restored crude versions of the sanitary functions, but there's not much division of labor down there. I remember coming out of anesthetic one time and overhearing a doctor refer to my previous privates with the word 'cloacae'. He probably thought it was pretty literate for a sawbones, but all I could think was that it just didn't sound very dainty."

Doc slowly raised his eyes to hers, met a defiant glare. He took a step toward her, but she started to bristle. He reached to embrace her, but she angrily knocked his arm away. He grabbed her upper arms and pulled her to him, over-riding her resistance. He crowded in on her, wrapped her in his arms and held him to him in a shuddering hug. Her anger soared and thrashed, then burned out into tears. After a moment of sobbing, he looked into her face.

"I love you, Jude," he almost whispered. "I've loved you all this time. That's what matters."

Her sobs broke into hysterical gasps. She pushed

134

away violently, breaking his hug. "Great idea, Doc," she yelled. "Love conquers all, right? You ever read 'Farewell to Arms'? Well here's a scoop: it wasn't his arms that were missing."

She jumped away from him as he reached for her again, bolting to the doorway. She stood there braced in the jamb, staring at him with a frozen expression. Her poise came back over her and she brushed off her shirt. "Is it okay with you if I get on with my career here without a lot of white lace and promises? I do just fine until somebody pops up to remind me I'm an incomplete. So can you do me one favor, Doc? As an old war buddy? Get the fuck out of my life and stay out?"

Doc stood, stricken, as she walked to the door in a precise, clipped stride. She turned, one hand on the jamb, and looked him right in the face. She smiled with a bittersweet affection. "Hey, soldier. Don't act like you never heard of anybody losing their cherry in combat. Way I hear it, you're a bit of a mess yourself. *C'est la guerre.*"

She stepped out of the doorway and Doc listened to every clipped, staccato stride down the hall. He was standing in the same place later when Jim Dandy looked in the door and stepped up to clasp his shoulder. "Man, I'm sorry Doc. I knew you had it, but not that bad."

"Aw, that was just for her benefit," Doc said in overtly fake bluff stuff. "So she wouldn't get all choked up. You know women."

"Not as many as I'd like."

"Help yourself to my share."

"You just gotta develop a taste for my type. High frequency, low fidelity, lotta wow and flutter."

"Woofers, or tweeters?"

"Hooters, my friend. Growlers. Knockers and heavers. I'm talking supercalifragiballistic here, the real nitty gritty gang bang. Let's go sniff something up, have a few laughs."

"Why the hell not?"

Jimmy stood, uncharacteristically quiet, for a long moment, regarding Doc's profile. "This shit ain't working this time, is it Doc? I get the feeling your heart's not in it."

"It's okay. Just play along and I'll fake it."

"Look here, amigo, remember back in the sixties..."

"They say if you remember the sixties you didn't do it right."

"Or didn't do enough. But remember that 'Make love, not war' jazz?

"Vaguely. I tried doing both, but had mixed results."

"What it was, they were just too young to know which was more dangerous. War you get over."

"So you know a thing or so about love?"

"Well, I hate to brag. But you're looking at the guy who, boo, boop a doop, who wrote the book of love.

"So what's it all about, Jimmy? I'd really, really like to know."

"Well, I'm gonna tell you Doc. Love is a drag, man. It's just a beautiful, beautiful drag."

"Figures. What isn't?"

"*Tunes*, baby! All you need is a little bit of soul, little magic of the music called rock and roll. Little shoop de boop, little bop and stroll."

"Well, we got invited to that concert tomorrow night."

"An' you watch, Bubba. I'm gonna set you up. Blind date. Which, no offense, is 'bout your only chance."

136

TWENTY-FOUR

You could tell from the next block that something was going inside. The street rocked with Afro-Cuban instrumental throb that just reeked of Miami After Hours, but all the Latinos in flashy formal, squiring hot women, getting out of posh cars and limos, weren't street players and definitely had tickets. A sprinkling of paparazzi and TV cams bobbled around the fringes on the sidewalk, but as likely to be scanning for known crime, drug and entertainment figures as anything to with the Cubano A-listers pressing to the doors, much less the featured entertainment inside the big hall. The entertainment in question being pretty graphically indicated by posters consisting of little but a head shot of a beaming but thoughtful Javier Perez.

Lukewarm attention turned to the latest stretch limo to sidle up to curb. One more huge white aircraft carrier with sunroofs, Caddy emblems hidden away, and probably galley slaves under the hood. The attention heightened somewhat when Doc stepped out, immediately followed by Jim Dandy offering a gentlemanly hand to the resplendent Sancha, whose exit could have filled up a soft-porn website by itself, and her outfit triggered a tug-of-war between Worst Dressed and Best Undressed lists. Honed professional observers scented crime, drug, and entertainment personnel all in one fell swoop. Jimmy and Doc fell in beside Sancha as she stilted across the sidewalk, her every exaggerated movement breaking hearts and itching trousers.

Behind them, a little ill-natured struggling freed Herman Moss to join the party. He got out the door, bandaged and *hors du combat,* resisting assistance from a tall, exactly built, black woman wearing an extremely sexy variation on a nurse ensemble. She smoothed his cummerbund and fussed with one of his bandages, but he jerked away and lumbered towards the hall.

The crowd parted before them as they moved towards lobby entrance. Doc and Herman practically gleamed in white dinner jackets with satin sashes and ties. Jimmy sported a tuxedo jacket and boiled shirt, a top hat, jungle print baggy shorts and alien tennis shoes. Sancha hung on his arm doing a Lupe Velez number in plummeting super-slinky, gathering eyeballs and flashbulbs in a haughty slither to the door. Jim's escorting hand was no longer so gentlemanly.

The religious culties that such flash crowds invariably draw surged around the far edges, nibbling their attention crust from the strays and stunned. The pushiest of the cults, brazenly accosting concert-goers with buckets and boxes marked with apocrypha and craving for donations, wore saffron robes and baseball caps bearing the logo of the Miami Dolphins. One of them spotted Jim, almost fell off his sandals, and beckoned his fellow flock to follow. Agitated and pointing, they ran to surround Jim Dandy as he prepared to enter the lobby. They bowed, scraped and salaamed their asses off in obvious awe, transcendently gassed when he waved a beneficent hand at them in passing.

The head cultie, who looked somewhat familiar to Doc, ran to Jimmy, bowed frantically, and pressed a fistful of money into his hand. Jim nonchalantly pocketed the alms, nimbly eluded their numinous rubbernecking, and stepped towards the lobby doors. A few bolder devotees attempted to kiss the hem of his garment, but Jim deftly sidestepped them, proclaiming, "Careful, sports fans, this is my class action suit. Why don't I catch y'all in the mosh pit?"

At the doors, Jim and Sancha turned to pose, Jim dragging Doc into the tableau by his elbow. They took a group bow the Manhattan Transfer would have envied, drawing a firestorm of flashes and whistles before ducking into the lobby. Grumbling, Moss and his "nurse" followed them, her starched while linen with no evident undergarments also copping a whistle or two.

Inside the huge glass doors, front and center before the sweeping jet-age stairways, the senior Perez held court. This was one of his biggest circuses ever, and the throng attending the sell-out were more motivated by stroking him than a sudden interest in classical music. Flanked by his dumpy wife and some rather clashingly obvious muscle, Perez accepted the hands, eyes and favor of Miami's Latino society. His wife smiled diffidently and anonymously, but Perez was pumped up like a fighting cock, so full of himself it was slopping over the top.

He looked up and scowled to see a Negro approaching him, but one look at Sancha dimmed his racial distastes. He swelled up even fuller at the sight of her, coming on point like a bird dog. His wife suddenly found previously unsuspected points of interest on the ceilings and walls as her husband simultaneously ogled Sancha and glowered at the bandaged black agent. Moss matched his glower and upped it, but said, "Yo Mister Perez, may I present Sanchita Cornelia Aduana del Valle, best known to you as 'Guantanamera'? "

Perez devoured her with eyes, grabbed her hand in both of hers and murmured, "After all these years of such loyalty, it's such a pleasure to meet you in the flesh."

"Yeah," Sancha commented idly, "It generally is."

Perez mumbled blandishments in Spanish as he moved in on Sancha, who countered it with a mixture of demure coquetry and smoldering sensuality.

Jim slid behind Doc and tapped him on the shoulder. "Couldn't findya a blind date, so I hadda settle for one that's outta her fuckin' mind."

He pointed to a stairway, which concealed all but the lower half of a gorgeous gown and some damn fine calves. A graceful descent of the stairway revealed more of the blind date, who was dressed like the satin Latins and coquetting behind a fan. She swept down the stairs and straight up to Doc, then tapped fan closed. None but Jude Mayfield, beautifully done up, tressed and bejeweled. Doc was too stunned even to stammer, but there was no need as Jude touched a gentle finger to his lips and girlishly murmured, "It's a lovely evening, don't spoil it by saying anything."

Doc glanced at Jimmy in wild surmise: Jimmy shrugged. "I ain' to proud to beg."

"And after a while," Jude beamed, "A girl will do just about anything to get rid of him. Isn't it about to begin?"

She held her arm out just so and Doc took it with something near the grace it deserved. Jim pried Sancha from the avid talons of Perez and she draped on his arm. The "nurse", who might have started resembling a very expensive call girl of the type a guy like Jim Dandy might have been able to locate, took Herman's arm and patted his wrist, drawing his hairy eyeball as they all six promenaded into the concert hall itself, trailing clouds of glamour, glory, and ersatz class.

A single spotlight lanced through the dark interior of the hall, isolating and sparkle-plating the slim figure of Javier Perez as he leaned back, critically examining his hands as they moved up the scales for the kill. His handsome face was perspiring, his wiry body seething with the fire of his playing, as he hunched into the complex, spasmodic finale.

Then the music stopped brutally and portentously as he slumped, hands by his side, and the dying echoes of the huge Steinway were drowned by applause from all sides. He looked out into the foot lights and waved affectionately to the first loge. Perez, senior, puffed up even more, his face softened with paternal love and pride. Then Javi drew himself up for another opus, his shoulders hunching forward, his finger pads hovering. There might have been some who looked askance at their programs, seeing nothing more listed, but the spotlight narrowed in and Javi launched into another opus.

He brushed the keys like a shy lover, a light and sweetly haunting air tinkling out onto the ready ears. They were ready to be soothed and seduced, relaxed and sighing. As he snapped to his feet, his knees knocking the bench over to crash dramatically on the floor behind him. In the shocked silence that ensued, he pounced on the piano, flailing away at a demented boogie-woogie.

In the loge, Perez *pere* stared in incredulous horror.

The spotlight widened, as if confused and shocked, and Javier danced all over the silver light. He slammed the keys, he leapt up and played while supported only by his flashing fingers. He dropped to a crouch and hammered the ivories with his elbows. He swung up like a movie cowboy mounting his nag, sitting on the music rest to play with both hands and feet. Every trick Jerry Lee and Elton ever pulled flashed by as he tore through his rampaging tune.

The audience stared, trapped in indecision whether to move to the compulsive beat or cower before the reaction of Perez himself as he seemed to be working up into advanced apoplexy.

The tension in the hall was palpable when Javi snapped forward from the waist, hammering out a final dischord with his forehead, then slammed the lid down on the keys and karate-chopped the ebony prop, allowing the lid to slam down with a clap of full-range doom. He threw a sweeping bullfighter bow, then stalked off the stage. The silence was intimidating, ominous. Until broken by Jim Dandy, whistling through his two little fingers and whooping. "Right on, cousin! Rockin roll! Rip it up! Boogie til ya puke, baby! Whoo. I taught that boy everything he knows that's worf a shit!"

He whipped out a lighter and held it up from his seat at the far end of Perez' loge. "Come on people, he exhorted, "Put your hands together for the kid. Get the cobs out and give it the hell up!"

Sporadically, almost timidly, the crowd began to clap and come to their feet. Jim kept on hoorahing them, holding his lighter overhead until other little flames came on around the dark room like fireflies. Perez, at his core completely a politician, picked up the drift and started to applaud wildly, gesturing to his entourage to respond in kind. At that, any restraint collapsed and the hall stomped and roared.

Jimmy swung his bulk from side to side, staring a "wave" which caught on and swept the hall, post Latino socialites getting into it, a galaxy of lighter flames swaying like a waltzing constellation above the claps and cheers.

Javier came back on stage, tearful; and jubilant, to take a feverish curtain call, gleaming and waving.

There is no question about an encore. He started out with a pompous quartet of notes, the famous Beethoven opening. Then suddenly slid into a raging rocker with a salsa inflection.

Sancha slid out of the Perez box like a jungle cat, presenting herself to be danced with. Jim took her up on it, swinging her into a scorching bop and stroll that showed off one hell of a lot of leg. Younger concert-goers were also slipping into the aisle to shake a leg. Ushers proved powerless to restore order, and not all that willing. Doc took Jude in a dance class stance, but immediately turned it into a swing step, spinning her out to an arm's reach, then back. She seemed reserved, but broke into a laugh at a particularly daring dip.

Herman and Big Nurse were also boogying their booties off--Frankenstein meets Queen Latifah.

Javier was having the time of his life, dark sunglasses appearing from nowhere, a prop for rocking his head like Ray Charles as he pounded it down.

Jim snapped his fingers at Sancha, gesturing at her panty line. She slipped out of her barely-mentionables with a move that practically collapsed several of the men around her, pulled them from under her clingy dress, and tossed them onto the stage. An elegantly coiffured doyen gasped at the flash of scarlet silk, then laughed and bent over, her hands going up under her designer gown. Sancha pinched a spray of roses from a stylish woman in the front row and pitched them onto the piano.

It was raining flowers and lingerie on stage. Javier caught a pair of Victoria's undies and wafted them near his face--to frenzied cheers--then placed them in his suit pocket like a handkerchief. Then he leaned into a salsa stomper with plenty of left hand, beating a musical path from Africa to Havana to Miami, bringing it all home as a fever in the night.

Linton Robinson

Author

Linton Robinson is a veteran, award-winning
writer and journalist with many years living in and
writing about Mexico, Cuba, and various borders.
To follow Lin and his increasing number of novels,
go to his website at LinRobinson.com or on
Twitter @LintonRobinson

The Doc Hardesty Novels

"Doc" Hardesty is a different kind of series hero.
Veteran of the worlds' wars, mercenary callings,
and hired gunnings, he works as a photographer
and seeks peace. He's a bit melancholy because
he seldom finds it.
A world adventurer given to dry, bitter-sweet kinds
of romance, Doc doesn't dominate his books, but
serves as a host for more spectacular allies.

A rotten governmental ploy leads
Doc across three continents in
search of a lost love. Livened no
end by Jimmy Dan Earl, legendary
rock and roll wildman. Jim Dandy
is the main reason this short novel,
converted from the screenplay, has
won so many fans.

The attraction
here is Dancy
Russell--the
beautiful, wild,
athletic, amoral
heiress kidnapped by a Mexican drug kingpin, but soon
taking over the gang as the men who love her end up dead.
Including Doc if he doesn't watch out.

BONUS CHAPTERS

Hopefully, you have enjoyed "Afro-Cuban Boogie Woogie" and wouldn't mind checking out more adventures of Doc and his crowd. A second book of this series (actually written first) is available on Kindle and SmashWords and you can read some excerpts from it below.

Here are a couple of excerpts from "For Your Damned Love", focusing on Dancy Russell. But don't worry, Doc comes through when called for.

In the excerpt from CHAPTER FIVE, Dancy is recovering from having been drugged--though not enough to keep her from shocking her kidnappers with spectacular violence--to find herself in their clutches. She handles it fairly well, to the chagrin of her current captor.

By the time the excerpt from CHAPTER THIRTEEN rolls around, the kidnapper is dead, Dancy is shacked up with his second in command--one of the more endearing and fearsome characters--and has corrupted *the narco-desperados* into robbing a bank of her choosing, culmination of what she terms here "Call-forwarding of The Wild".

For more information, or to purchase book in this series, we invite you to visit:

http://linrobinson.com

http://adorobooks.com

FOR YOUR DAMNED LOVE --
CHAPTER FIVE

Dancy came around slowly, her awareness seeping up through a residue of fatigue and drugs. As she recalled her adventures before losing consciousness, she decided to take it all very deliberately, snoozing and recovering her strength before making any moves. By the time she was fully awake she had recovered her vitality and felt fine except for a very nasty stomach. You bastards don't have good enough drugs to dent my hateful good health, she thought.

She had gotten accustomed to the swaddling of an expensive featherbed, the touch of expensive silk sheets on her bare skin, the soft murmur of piano concertos, and a distant hum of motor by the time she opened her eyes to scan the tiny stateroom. Because she was obviously on some sort of yacht. Elegant workmanship and fine materials had been lavished on creating the look of a Pullman car from the twenties. The colors were ebony and silver, the style a sort of art deco/disco, and the tone all lush, plush and hushed. Enough black velvet to paint Elvis' whole family, Dancy she thought. Since she saw no sign of more drugs, guns or strange men, she leaned over on one elbow and teased back the heavy drapes above the bed. She'd fully expected chromed portholes offering views of some freebooter's harbor, but instead found herself staring down ten thousand feet at an unbroken arc of smooth blue ocean.

Well, she thought, I guess yachts are just pretty passé for the modern pirate. Maybe I'll hail the stewardess or cabin boy for a couple of those tiny bottles of grog. Some honey-roasted cashews. With that thought, she glanced at the ceiling above the bed and saw that there actually was a call button. She pushed it firmly, then arranged her hair on the pillow and the sleek black comforter across her breasts. Captured heroines should look the part, she thought, or the extras might get out of hand.

It didn't exactly amaze her when Armando Lios Leyva stepped through the cabin door wearing black slacks and blazer and carrying a tray with a crystal snifter and bottle of Armagnac. Dancy gave him a nod and said, "Well, this is more like it. I much prefer the first class rape."

Armando moved over beside the bed and pulled a jumpseat out of the wall. He sat down, handed her the snifter and splashed brandy in it for her, "It's not exactly a rape, Dancy."

"You drug me, have me carried off, put me in bed naked, and fly me away from my husband. What would you call it...leaving the scene of an accident?"

Armando chuckled, then gave her serious look as she sipped the brandy. "I'd call it more of an opportunity for both of us. I get the chance to win you. You get the chance for an adventure."

Dancy looked a little skeptical, "I've found when you guys start talking about adventure and winning me it's time for a gal to start guarding her virtue."

"I hear you guard what virtue you have very impressively," Armando grinned, "But I'm not here to force you into anything. I'm not offering you some cheap affair; I'm offering you a chance to share my world with me. I think you'll find it a very rich life."

Dancy idly pulled back a strand of hair and said, "Actually, the life I had was fairly rich."

Her response left Armando nonplussed. He was

2

used to impressing women with his looks, physique, and wealth. To this one, that was all part of the daily drag. He had never met a woman that hadn't been turned on by the plane itself. Dancy Russell didn't even notice. In fact, she gave the impression that she was politely concealing the fact that everything about the set-up was hopelessly gauche or second-rate. He felt a hot spasm of visceral desire that went beyond her face and body: he would impress this bitch. He would impress her to death.

He leaned closer to look her right in the face, his voice dropping into a sonorous seriousness. "Dancy, we are two of a kind. I want to show you that we belong together. You're a woman who demands the very best, I'm a man who can make remarkable things happen. As you have seen. I can be more of a man to you than that clown of a husband. I can be more man to you than you've ever known."

Dancy made a wishy-washy gesture with her free hand, "Well, you all keep saying that. And God knows I keep hoping, but..."

Armando slowly reached out to touch her wrist. He said, "Do you know what I think? I think it's a long time since you've been surprised." Dancy looked at him quickly, thinking, *Touché*. Armando caught the glance and held it, saying "I think I will surprise you."

"You're doing pretty good, so far."

Armando found that the most gratifying thing he'd heard in some time. He allowed himself to drink in the vision of Dancy's tawny face against the slick black pillows. The puffy comforter slid down her breasts a little as she leaned against her head against the window, hints of pinkish aureoles appearing. She craned her neck to look back behind the plane, as though trying to see what she was leaving behind. He was ready to calm her entreaties and protests when she

3

turned back to face him; to reassure her kindly or refuse her implacably. What she said was, "Could you get him to fly lower? Like right over the tips of the waves?"

FOR YOUR DAMNED LOVE --
CHAPTER THIRTEEN

Dancy slid into the bank with a lax smile, her eyes and gun sweeping the room for challenge. The line of customers still stretched entirely around the inside of the bank, but now they all had their hands clasped behind their heads and their eyes fastened on Santiamen and Ramos, who looked quite capable of shooting them down for lunch meat. The two pretty young tellers were by the barred door of the vault, quivering like frightened mares in the lecherous clutches of Maldonado and Regalado. Martillo was having a heart-to-heart with the branch manager, who seemed very co-operative, as well as flabbergasted by Martillo's mask.

He was the only masked member of the gang. since he was the one readily recognizable. Dancy had chosen the mask from the remains of Armando's huge collection. It was carved wood, featuring the bearded face, elaborately curled hair, and glaring gaze of a biblical patriarch--but with a large red scorpion passed through his head, curving, steel-spiked tail coming out of one ear and the evil agate eyes from the other. It wouldn't have looked half so surrealistic, though, without Martillo's buff Stetson perched on top of it. Martillo had groused, "It's just some stupid Indio superstitious thing."

"It's perfect," Dancy had told him over his

4

understandable objections, "Nobody will remember anything else about any of us."

"I think they might remember somebody looking like Faye Dunaway," he'd said. But Dancy was rooting among the other masks. "Too bad they don't have some kind of codpiece," she mumbled, "A nice beaded combat dildo with lobster claws or something."

Martillo had to have "codpiece" and "dildo" explained. He grimaced, "How about if I just run in with a naked hard-on and a gun in each hand?"

"I like it," Dancy crowed. "A lot. But not this time. You've gotta keep back something for the sequel."

Martillo had made his preliminary announcements in both Spanish and English, and the Mexican customers looked very cowed by his remarks and the cavalier display of firepower. Some foreigners, however, were just disgruntled, arrogant and ignorant enough to put up some guff. One bandy-legged, barrel-chested old fart with tufts of white hair sticking out his ears like a goat and "Navy Chief, Retired" practically tattooed on his forehead, rolled up to Ramos saying, "Look here, Peedro." He thought of himself as a local hand because he'd owned a house in Peritas for twenty years, although he spoke no Spanish and knew no locals; that he was a shrewd investor because he had $30,000 in the BanComer at 95% interest, although that rate didn't even match the peso's inflation; and that he had a natural authority over Mexican riffraff, although nobody had understood his barked orders around the town and only humored him out of a pious regard for the feeble-minded.

He demanded that they get their butts out of the bank and quit pestering American bigod citizens. Ramos grinned, stuck the tip of a machine gun in the old salt's mouth, pointed at his massive gold Omega, snapped his fingers for it. "What are you gonna do,

Julio, shoot an American citizen?" the old guy cawed around the gun barrel.

"Not at all," Dancy Russell snapped from behind him. As he turned, glad to deal with somebody intelligent enough to speak American, she went on. "We're going slap your silly face." She gave a full backhand swing that snapped through the bank like a pistol shot, almost knocking the geezer off his feet.

"Then we'll kick you in your used-up old nuts." She did that so well he didn't even cry out, just hit the floor unconscious.

"Then I'll just sit on your face while I go through your pockets and decide whether to cut off your shriveled old pecker and toast it over a campfire." She plunked down on his face and looked around the other tourists. "Is there anyone else who doesn't understand that they should give us everything they have and hope to God it's enough?"

There was a rapid tattoo of purses, wallets and watches hitting the floor. Dancy bounced up, curtsied and said, "Very good, now for short arm inspection and pap smears."

The rudimentary vault had been locked only with a key, which had been forthcoming very fast when Torres and Santiamen loomed over the manager. Regalado and Maldonado whooped inside, rifling stacks of cash and documents and tossing them into sacks like demented Santas gone way bad. Torres looked at the deposit boxes sadly. "If only we could get into those. That's where they keep the real money, the virgin wool."

Santiamen agreed, "Gold," he rumbled, "And dollars. Not these damned pesos."

"Well, I don't see any way to get into them other than drilling the locks one by one. Damn shame."

Santiamen grunted, spit eloquently on the miserly little boxes, and lumbered out of the vault at Torres' heels.

Maldonado and Regalado were stunned by this frustrating information and stared at the boxes in a mixture of awe and indignation. "Next time we'll just blow the whole mother and pick up what's left," Regalado predicted.

Maldonado could really see the wisdom in that. "The boss should get one of those helicopters."

Regalado's eyes widened at his remembrance of what the helicopter had done to the mansion, "Yeah, a motherless helicopter. You said it, *compa*. He wagged an admonitory finger at the offending boxes, "Next time we'll bust your mother and take a look up your skirts, you little *chingamadres*."

Meanwhile Dancy was having more luck and good clean fun with the unsecured valuables about the persons of customers. She snatched a gaudy necklace off the leather-skinned neck of a ridiculously over-tanned woman wearing large round sunglasses and a T-shirt with a big red valentine and the words "I" and "Detroit".

"Tacky enough, but maybe worth something if the stones are real." Dancy nonchalantly draped the necklace around her neck with five others. "You should know better than to wear stuff like that on the street. I mean, Detroit, for God's sake."

"And who the hell are you, you little bitch?" the woman snorted, "An appraiser?"

Dancy turned to Martillo in astonishment, "See how soon they forget?" She turned back to the woman and stuck the chopper barrel into a sun-baked nostril as she introduced herself, "I'm Patty Fuckin' Hearst. And introducing my merry men, the Semiautomatic Libertine Army. We make our money the old-fashioned way. We kill people and take it."

Her crusty toughness cracked, the woman made an involuntary start with her hand, which brought Dancy's eye to her large diamond solitaire. She grabbed the hand and whistled in admiration.

"No, that's my wedding ring," the woman wailed, "Thirty seven years!"

"I'd feel sorry for your husband, but he apparently had enough money to spare him some of the horror," Dancy commiserated.

The woman jerked back into her normal vitriolic mode and spat out, "It won't come off anyway."

Dancy held the finger captive while reaching out towards Ramos and snapping her fingers. "Forceps," she barked, "Scalpel."

Terrified, the woman yelled, "No, no, wait!" and started trying to push the ring off. Her struggles and sweating increased as Ramos sauntered over, groping in the pockets of his coveralls. She was at the point of fainting when he extracted a pair of side-cutters, murmured "*Con su permiso,*" and snipped off the ring to present it to Dancy with a courtly flourish.

Dancy started off, admiring the ring, then stepped back, grabbed the woman's sunglasses and put them on. "We're just gangsters, lady," she explained, "Gangsters of love."

Nobody else gave Dancy the slightest trouble as she stripped their purses and pockets. While the Mexican customers kept nervous eyes on Santiamen as armed bear and Martillo as avatar of the Scorpion God protocols, the gringos unanimously rolled their eyes to follow Dancy; silently apprehensive as she did Paula Abdul steps around the lobby, cramming their stuff in her bag while singing to herself, "Money, it's a crime..."

The only hitch was the manager. The man had been

a shambles from the first, sweating and trembling. But when Santiamen pulled him to his feet and told him to be a good little hostage or else, the man turned gray and grabbed for his chest, nearly fainting. Both of the tellers gasped and the shorter, prettier one tried to run to help him, brought up short by Maldonado's arm across her chest and fingers around her right tit. At her first movement Ramos had reflexively jerked his gun up to cover her, but she dared it, sobbing, "No, no, his heart...his surgery...oh, please don't!"

The girl shrugged free of Maldonado's groping and brushed past Ramos' gun, running to where the manager had slumped back into his chair and falling on her knees beside him. "You can't take him, you've hurt him enough. Take me instead."

Annoyed, Martillo stepped over to the desk and tore open the sweat-stained white shirt. There was no mistaking the shiny red scar and raw stitch marks up the sternum. The man was deeply shaken, but licked his lips and said, "No. I'm okay. Leave the girls alone."

Impressed by these sudden flourishes of courage and devotion, Martillo turned to Santiamen and ordered, "He'd just die on us. Take the girls instead." The big man nodded as though he'd already assumed that much, gently pulled the sobbing teller off the man, and motioned Regalado to take the other girl over to the door. At the sight of the tall girl's pale, shocked face and shaky step the manager stirred in his chair, begging Martillo, "No, please. Take me and leave the girls. They're just kids. I'll be all right."

Martillo growled that all the bravery was very touching but the girls were hostages and that was that. He leaned his hideous mask down into the manager's face, as though menacing him, and said in a low, soft voice, "Don't worry about the girls. No harm will come to them. I promise you that." The manager stared at the grotesque persona in amazement, as though it had just occurred to him there was a human behind it.

As Santiamen slung his gun and gathered up most of the bags, Maldonado and Regalado hustled the girls to the door, restraining their more overt feel-copping under Ramos' frown. Dancy finished gathering wallets and glanced at the girls. "Good thinking, boys," she congratulated them. "Man doesn't live by bread alone."

As they formed up in the door for their dash to the trucks, Ramos and Torres covering the customers for their withdrawal, she frowned and said, "But isn't it more traditional to throw the women over your shoulders?"

"We're robbing the bank," Martillo snapped, "Not sacking the town."

"Ah, right," she shrugged, "One step at a time."

As the gang burst out of the bank Dancy, instead of getting in the back of the truck with the hostages as planned, untied Torres' horse and swung up on it as the truck doors all slammed. Only Morales and Torres, at the wheels of the getaway trucks, saw her. She had the pony figured out before it took five steps; young, poor quality, skittish enough for about anything. She took him in hand and headed him out into the street.

As the trucks pulled away from the curb Martillo saw her cutting across towards the park. Torres saw her too and braked the panel so suddenly that Morales bumped its rear end with the pickup. The whole gang watched Dancy canter over to the park and jump the three-foot white stone fence that supported the huge gilt bust of Padre Hidalgo. She cantered right to the center and up the stairs of the little bandstand as the whole town stared in universal wonder. Rearing the horse and spinning it around, she triggered a burst of machine gun fire into the air then smoothly recovered as the
10

terrified horse tore off the platform and back into the street. At a full, dusty gallop she waved her hat, then scaled it away to let her hair blow free. She plunged past the taco venders, sidewalk stalls, and gawking *campesinos*, firing at the signs that stuck out above the rooftops. She punched 9mm holes through the ads for "La Isleña" liquors, "El Nayar" hardware, and "Luna de Miel" bar as she charged out towards the highway.

Torres was already accelerating. It was only his first bank job and evidently a highly unorthodox one at that, but he knew better than to stick around admiring the craziness of a *gringa*. He said, "*Jefe*?"

"Follow her," Martillo said. "We'll catch her on the highway."

From the back, Ramos said, "Not until she's out of bullets, I hope."

She was waiting at the crossing. She jumped off the horse, fired a last burst into the air, and yelled at Peritas in general, "Too rad for you!"

"You could have just called the police and saved bullets," Martillo grumped as she hopped in the panel's rear doors.

"I think they got the word as soon as we were out the door, sugar. I just couldn't resist. I mean how often does a girl get the chance to shoot up a town?"

Martillo said nothing as the two trucks blasted up the grade towards the hills to the south, making it clear he didn't care for the cinematic school of bank jobs. But Regalado and Maldonado, sitting like tail gunners in the back of the pickup, approved enthusiastically. "I told him," Maldonado swore, "We should have done it on horseback. How would the cops catch us if we're in the jungle, not on the road?"

"That *bandida* mother has got it right," Regalado

agreed, "On horseback, all balls and a cloud of gunsmoke--*a todo madre.*" The gang had almost forgotten her as a sex object: she had big balls, end of story.

It only took the gang twenty minutes to reach the first turnoff, and another fifteen to climb to the end of the dirt road where they had stashed the hijacked bakery truck at a tiny rancho. While they hastily transferred the hostages and money sacks into the step van, Martillo and Ramos debated a change of plans on the hostages. They had planned to keep the manager with them until the last minute, then abandon him on the treacherous, twisting road they would take over the mountain to Bahia Mantechen. But the tall girl was so obviously in deep hysterical shock that Dancy felt sorry for her, even apprehensive that she might drop dead on them. They decided to leave her at the rancho, where the Señora clucked sympathetically and started cooking her something.

They loaded the other girl into the truck and crept back down to the highway, turning back towards the north. The big truck was painted with the name and design of Bimbo, Mexico's largest bread company, and was therefore virtually invisible on the road. Dancy hadn't missed the chance to pose for several pictures taken by a recently stolen camera; mugging with guns and bandoliers under the big Bimbo logo. She hadn't bothered to explain the pictures to Martillo, or her burst of laughter at first sight of the truck. "It's a gringo thing," was all she'd say.

Ramos and Santiamen drove the getaway trucks down almost to the highway, then out into a fallow tobacco field, where they punctured their gas tanks and set them on fire. Dancy and Torres watched out the rear windows as the Bimbo truck drove off and were rewarded by seeing both trucks explode into roiling balls of red flame.

Martillo drove, since he was the only one who'd been masked. As they tooled right through the Peritas crossing, everyone ducked but Martillo, who cut his eyes down the main street of the town to gauge the milling around and count the trucks full of excited men. They pulled along sedately to the cutoff just past Las Varas, then headed up into the mountains on a road so sinuous, rutted, and overgrown as to be almost impassable. But they could squeeze past, and the road would eventually lead them over to Santa Cruz on Mantechen Bay, where Martillo's Buick and a van were garaged in a sugar cane barn.

The posse would find the burned vehicles pretty quickly and start searching the web of roads to the south. By then they'd have left the bread truck in the barn, where it would sit for a month until the cane harvest. They would leave the pretty teller at a tiny farm commune halfway over the hill, where it would be at least three days before she could get out. Then they would zip straight up to the main highway, come through Tepic from the north, and be safely home by nightfall.

In the back of the lurching Bimbo truck, Dancy had been studying the frightened bank teller. "You know," she told her, "You're not a bad-looking kid."

"She can't understand you," Martillo said from the front seat.

"Oh, she understands," Dancy said, "Female vanity is a universal language." She leaned across the scared *Mexicana*, who twisted around to face her, pushing back against Regalado's shoulder. She slid a fingernail under the chain of the small gold crucifix and dangled it teasingly against the girl's sweating cleavage. The girl gasped and Morales turned around to see what was going on, to be rewarded when Dancy said, "Lemme see something here," and tore the girl's blouse open. She eyed the soft, prominent mounds quivering in black lace cups. The girl was at the point of desperation but froze, eyes and nostrils flaring wide, when Dancy pulled out Armando's black and silver switchblade and snicked it open. Martillo glanced back at the sound and the truck yawed at his surprise, "What the devil are you doing?" he yelled.

"Just inspecting the booty," Dancy drawled. "Well, the boobies, really. You just watch the road; this is girl talk."

She slid the blade under the bra between the cups, then twisted it and whipped it away from the girl's ribs, slashing the bra and letting her breasts tumble free. Carefully closing the knife and pocketing it, she reached for the bra cups. The girl's hands fluttered up, but fell away at Dancy's trademark glare. Dancy gathered the lapels of the navy blazer and white blouse in both hands and hunched them down over her shoulders. The whole gang was extremely interested by this time and Regalado, looking over the girl's shoulder and feeling her shivering against him, was starting to think the *gringa* was the greatest thing that ever happened. Brushing the cups aside, she pulled both breasts out and cupped them gently. They were quite lovely; young, pale and firm with very dark aureoles and nipples standing out in sheer fear. "Well now, honey, this is just about pretty titty city. Right, boys?"

Martillo was pretty interested himself, even though he needed to keep a certain amount of attention on barreling the bread truck down the snaking, flaking road. He kept glancing into the mirror, not sure if he was more concerned with the girl's tits or Dancy's behavior.

"Dancy?" he finally asked, "Are you enjoying

14

yourself?"

"I sure am, lover." Dancy was almost giggling, "I've always wanted to do that. Just check it out, you know? See if they're all they're pushed up to be. Haven't you?"

"Holy Virgin," Martillo said, "Don't hurt her, she's just a poor working girl."

"I wouldn't think of it," Dancy said. She was holding the girl's breasts up as proud as if she'd grown them herself from a seed packet. She was savoring the girl's terror, her power over all the world's nice young things. She held the girl's eye like a cobra, examining her. Was she a virgin? A Catholic? A hypocritical little bitch who'd damn her for sex and murder out of wedlock? Probably. She softened, sighed. She released the girl, patted a breast in a friendly manner. "Very nice, sweetheart. Tender vittles. But get a little more upthrust here, a smaller cup size, and don't fasten this button." She pulled the blouse back together, holding it to get the décolleté look she recommended. She made the girl hold the torn blouse, then fished in her bag for a mirror and showed the girl what she meant. God knows what the girl thought--probably that gang rape by outlaws was apparently even weirder than she'd been imagining.

Dancy took a long look at the girl holding her tits, a portrait of sexy helplessness that had Morales so hard he could barely maintain his position twisted around over the front seat. She reached into one of the duffle bags and said, "Now let's see if we can salvage that make-up."

The next time Martillo could glance back to see what sort of jolly surprises his girl was doing to his hostage in front of his gang in the middle of his getaway, she was sorting through a fistful of cosmetics.

"Where did you get that stuff?" he asked her, since he distinctly remembered scotching the drug store stop.

"Oh, all those cows had tons of it in their purses with the money and jewelry."

"You were stealing make-up during the bank robbery?"

"Well, it was pretty obvious *you* weren't going to buy me any."

Martillo shook his head and muttered, "I'll bet Faye Dunaway didn't bother stealing mascara and eye shadow."

Dancy ignored his confusion of actress with role, "Well no, but who has cheekbones like her?"

"You don't need make-up, *Bandida*. You don't need clothes. You don't need money."

"Well, let's not forget our guest, huh? In the States when you get taken hostage you end up on TV."

Martillo gave up, but the boys in the back maintained a certain level of interest as Dancy searched among the little tubes and compacts, held the bank girl's chin in her hand as she turned her head critically, then started wiping off her blue eye shadow and heavy mascara. "There's a difference between foxes and raccoons, honey," she said as she started painting a new face on the girl, who seemed to relax a little under her grooming. "The whole secret of subtlety is feathering; you shouldn't be able to tell where the stuff ends yourself."

By the time they reached the commune, the girl looked beautiful (if a little pale and shaky). Taking a last stroke with a fader, Dancy dusted her hands triumphantly and handed the girl the mirror. She was shocked, then became engrossed in studying her face, trying to memorize the effects and study out the techniques. Regalado and Maldonado enthusiastically applauded the effect, but maintained a somewhat closer scrutiny of those sweet round tits poorly confined by the ripped blouse and slashed bra.

When they dropped her out in front of the cane huts, Dancy gave her a good-bye kiss on the cheek, then looked her right in the eye. "Now don't tell anybody anything about any of this, or I'll come look you up, hear?"

Martillo translated and the girl shook her head violently, and continued after the bread truck loafed off down the washed-out road. She was very sure she wanted no further part of Dancy Russell. That bitch was crazy mean. A real gift for cosmetics, though.

If you liked "Afro-Cuba Boogie Woogie" and want to read "For Your Damned Love" or other cool titles by Linton Robinson, check his website
LinRobinson.com
Or the publisher's site at AdoroBooks.com
Or sign up for the newsletter at AdoroBooks.com/Mail

0 1341 1573370 8

CPSIA information can be obtained at www.ICGtesting.com
Printed in the USA
LVOW04s2304081214

417908LV00013B/238/P

9 781469 983929